The Dead Game

"It's a game my sister played at a retreat once," Linnie said. "The Dead Game. Everyone had an assigned target. And each player was a target, too. So while you were trying to 'kill' your target, someone else was trying to 'kill' you. The last one left alive was the winner."

She glanced at Jackson. He looked interested. So did Ming.

"A kind of bloodless vengeance," Jackson muttered.

Also in the
Point Horror series:

Look out for:

Point Horror

THE DEAD GAME

A. Bates

SCHOLASTIC

Scholastic Children's Books,
Scholastic Publications Ltd,
7-9 Pratt Street, London NW1 0AE, UK

Scholastic Inc.,
730 Broadway, New York, NY 10003, USA

Scholastic Canada Ltd,
123 Newkirk Road, Richmond Hill,
Ontario, Canada L4C 3G5

Ashton Scholastic Pty Ltd,
P O Box 579, Gosford, New South Wales,
Australia

Ashton Scholastic Ltd,
Private Bag 1, Penrose, Auckland,
New Zealand

First published by Scholastic Inc. 1993
This edition published by Scholastic Publications Ltd. 1994

Copyright © Auline Bates 1992

ISBN 0 590 55384 4

Printed by Cox & Wyman Ltd, Reading, Berks

10 9 8 7 6 5 4 3 2

*To Grover, who will never read this book,
and to Shirin and Wesley Grover, who will . . .
with thanks, love, and hope.*

THE DEAD GAME

Chapter 1

"Almost," Linnie said glumly.

She stuffed a piece of pizza crust into her milk carton.

The background noise — trays banging on table-tops, and several hundred voices complaining, joking, talking — went on all around her, ignored as she focused on her thoughts.

"Almost what?" Jackson asked.

He grabbed Linnie's milk carton and looked in the top. "I could have eaten that," he said sadly.

Linnie barely heard him. She frowned, stabbing her potato triangle with her fork, rubbing it back and forth in the ketchup on her tray as she worked at putting her thoughts into words.

She felt Jackson's hopeful stare and glanced up. "Oh, sorry. Here." She handed him the triangle, fork and all. "I almost had a good senior year," she explained, wiping her fingers on a napkin. "It was almost fun. It was almost memorable."

She wadded her napkin. "I'm almost glad I was here."

"You're disasterizing," Ming told her.

"I'm what?"

"Making a mountain out of a molehill," Ming said, tossing her dark hair back. "Maybe you aren't going to get an A in Studio. Maybe you're not going to be world-famous for your ceramic pots. That doesn't make the whole year a disaster. One class, maybe. But not the whole year."

"It makes my whole career plan a disaster!" As soon as she said the words, Linnie wished she could grab them back. Ming's disappointment was much worse than hers, and she'd hardly said a word about it.

"It's been a fine year for both of us," Ming said firmly. "And finally we're almost out of here. Out of Hollander High is where we've wanted to be since tenth grade, right? So we're doing great."

She sounds like she's giving a pep talk, Linnie thought. All that fake enthusiasm. But who is she trying to pep up — herself or me? She glanced thoughtfully at her friend, ignoring the people who stopped by to say hello to Jackson and offer any lunch they had left over. Jackson usually ate three lunches — one that he bought, two that were donated piecemeal — so the steady stream of offerings was commonplace.

Ming's earlier words hung unspoken over the table. *Graduating number three means nothing. It's not valedictorian. It's not salutatorian. It's nothing.* That was all Ming had said about the situation, and she'd said it back in January when Austin and Adler had transferred to Hollander and Ming's class rank plummeted immediately from first to third place.

Linnie said, "Maybe a meteorite will fall out of the sky and smash both the transfer twins in one crashing blow."

Ming gave a small grin, but it was only a fraction of her usual smile.

She's really hurting, Linnie thought, feeling helpless as she watched her sober-eyed, too-quiet friend. I've never been number one, but I know how it feels to be cut down!

"Maybe my real problem is I never had a real problem before," Ming said. "So when this hit, I didn't have any experience. I'm still kind of numb and it's been, what? Most of the semester?"

"Seems like forever," Jackson said.

"I've been thinking about it," Ming went on. "I realized how easy I've had it all my life. Getting good grades was never hard for me, and I'm naturally athletic. Making friends has always been easy because I'm not shy and I always liked everybody."

"Even Austin and Adler?" Jackson asked.

"I was talking past tense," Ming said. "No, I do not like the transfer twins. My point was I'm not handling this well. I think if someone had transferred here who had really worked hard for their grades . . . I think I'd feel better. At least I'd know they'd earned it. It's just so hard when Austin and Adler — well . . ." Her voice trailed off. "I think it's really sinking in now. Once the numbness wears off, it hurts."

Linnie stared at her lunch tray, empty except

for ketchup smears and a crinkled straw paper. It's not fair, she thought. If Hollander High doesn't offer Advanced Placement and Honors courses, why do they give extra rating points to people who take them somewhere else? Why is my friend hurting, and Austin and Adler, the cheats, are doing just fine?

Jackson licked his fingers. "I heard they researched," he told Ming. "The story I heard is they were ranked number eight and number ten at their prep school so their folks went looking for a place like Hollander — a place that has a good reputation but doesn't offer AP or Honors classes."

"Which automatically guarantees top ranking to anybody who just happens to have a bunch of AP classes on their transcripts," Linnie added. "And that stinks!"

"It's clever." Jackson crumpled his milk carton and tossed it into the bin across from the table. "So simple. Wonder why my folks didn't think of it."

Ming grinned again, a little wider this time. "Jackson, you wouldn't know an Honors course if it sat in your lap. The story is true, by the way. I heard Austin bragging. He and Adler think it's funny. Their parents are rich enough to move anywhere, and they picked here for A and A's final semester just so the boys can take top honors. Austin will graduate number one, and Adler is number two."

And you're number three, Linnie thought grimly. Not valedictorian. Not salutatorian. Nothing.

Jackson sighed. "Maybe we could manufacture a meteorite," he said. "We could spend evenings after track practice on the roof of the school building it, and when it's big enough to do mortal damage, Bam! We just roll it over the edge — at the exact moment the A and A boys are walking by, of course."

"That could be fun," Ming said, sounding less glum.

Linnie had smoothed out her napkin and was staring at it. I should have guessed, she thought. She's been so quiet lately. I should have known what was bothering her. The closer graduation gets, the worse it's going to hurt.

She felt Jackson's eyes on her and looked up. "What?" she asked. "Can I shred my napkin or do you want to eat that, too?"

"Go ahead and shred," Jackson told her. "I'm full for now."

"Thank you." Linnie solemnly tore a strip off the edge of her napkin, then a second one.

"I think we should do *something*," Jackson announced. "Something as nasty and underhanded as what they did."

"That's not possible," Linnie said.

"It's too late to transfer somewhere, even if I wanted to," Ming said. "And first I'd have to look for another school with no Honors classes and where no one already has a 4.0 grade point, which I might be willing to do if that meant getting even with Austin and Adler. But it wouldn't mean that. I'd just be hurting someone else. That would be pointless. If I were going to hurt someone, I'd want it to be the transfer twins."

"I didn't mean pull the same trick they did," Jackson said. "I just meant there has to be something we could do."

"All that's left is to hope someone kills them," Ming pointed out. "And soon. They're here. They have a higher grade-point average than I can ever get. It's over. They win. There wasn't even a battle. I lost without a fight."

"Actually," Linnie said slowly, "that's not a bad idea."

"What isn't?" Ming asked.

"Killing them," Linnie said.

Jackson and Ming looked doubtful, as if they weren't certain they'd heard right.

"Ax them, ice them, knock them off," Linnie said. "Bump them off. Chop." She made a chopping motion with her hand against the edge of the table.

Ming laughed uneasily. "You're kidding, right?" She and Jackson both turned to stare at Linnie.

Linnie tore off another shred of napkin and shook her head. "Nope," she said. "Death. I'm completely serious. It's the perfect solution."

Chapter 2

The pottery studio with its wheels and kilns and clay-stained tables was in the farthest corner of the school from the lunchroom, and Linnie hustled. Her art teacher was great, but she had the traditional artistic temperament and her pet peeve was people who were late to *her* class.

Linnie could recite the tirade from memory. "Nothing is more important than art. Artists may forget to eat, to sleep, to breathe, even, but they do not forget to come to class. On time!"

She did make it on time — barely — and spent the class alternately muttering at the vase that wouldn't soar artistically into being, and grinning as she remembered the expressions on Ming's and Jackson's faces as she'd left them in the lunchroom.

They'd mirrored each other, looking shocked, horrified, disbelieving, and just a tiny bit excited.

Linnie hadn't explained her idea, had suggested, instead, that they meet in the parking lot right after school to discuss it.

She turned her thoughts back to her vase. "It

just won't GO," she moaned to the teacher, who had paused at her table.

"Because you don't have any concentration to-day," the teacher replied, eyeing the vase critically. "Your fingers are like sausages poking at the clay."

Stung, Linnie stared at her hands, feeling clumsy. People do that to me, she thought. They find all my little sore spots and push on them. Just like my sister. Now I'm afraid to touch the clay. Maybe I'm not an artist at all. Artists have a different vision; I have . . . sausage fingers.

The teacher moved on to Brenda at the next table, murmuring a few words that, to Linnie, sounded like encouragement. But Brenda started crying. "You're right!" she yelled. She lifted her hand, made a sudden fist, and smashed her vase. "It was no good!" She raised clay-muddied hands and covered her face.

Oh, that was a good touch, Linnie thought, her lips compressing in disgust. Very carefully done. I wish I'd thought of it. It'll take her all of three minutes to dab the clay off her face and redo her lipstick. If she'd happened to touch a single hair on her head during her little fit I'd have been more impressed since that would have been a lot harder to fix!

She watched the teacher as she comforted Brenda, murmuring soothingly.

Now she'll get an A for her artistic temperament, Linnie thought, poking at her own vase. And she won't even have a project to turn in. I'll turn in a decent vase and get a C for sausage fingers. We'd better build a big meteorite because it's got to have room for Brenda under it, too.

Then she brightened. We don't have to limit ourselves to Austin and Alder! We can make up a hit list.

She laughed aloud, sobering almost instantly at the teacher's startled, hopeful stare.

No, I did not have a burst of artistic inspiration, she thought in silent answer to the teacher's look.

Her fingers molded the clay, feeling the cool dampness, the graininess, the way the clay responded to her touch. I love clay, she thought. It's so clean and fresh, like a baby, ready to be whatever I make it. I am the creator and the clay follows my thoughts and my hands.

The wheel spun and her fingers worked. The sides of the vase flared upward, forming into a graceful shape that reminded Linnie of an urn.

Maybe I did get inspired, she thought, watching the urn take shape. A hit list. Austin, Adler, and Brenda. I'd put my sister on it, too, but she lives too far away.

She grinned, admiring her urn, smiling over it at Brenda.

Chapter 3

Jackson and Ming were not waiting for her in the parking lot as they usually did when Linnie arrived after school. She waited, but it was not until she had given up and started walking home that she saw them, coming toward her.

Jackson, tall and muscular, stood nearly a foot taller than Ming. He walked with the aggressive gait of a defensive back on the football team, which he was. Ming, looking frail and tiny beside him, walked with the light and graceful step of a dancer, which she was not. She played volleyball, basketball, and was on the summer softball team, but she often said her dance skills had gotten stuck on basic fast and basic slow.

They both looked wary. And determined.

"Can't do it," Jackson said firmly, before Linnie had a chance to say anything. "And we can't let you do it, either. I can almost believe they deserve it, but I can't let it happen."

"You idiots!" Linnie said, laughing. "Is that why you're late? You've been trying to figure out how to stop me from killing people? I can't believe you took me seriously! I thought you understood . . . well, how could you? I didn't explain I meant a game. I just . . ."

She couldn't help laughing at the embarrassment and relief on their faces. "You guys are too much!" she said. "After all the years you've known me you actually think I could turn into a murderer? You know I don't like blood. It's messy. Anyway, I've got a much more practical idea. Come on, let's go get a taco or something and I'll explain."

The taco stand was half a block up from the school, on the other side of the street, and after ordering, they took their food back across the street to the park that adjoined the school grounds.

"Let's eat down by the river," Ming suggested. She led the way to where the river lined the north edge of the park. The banks had been fenced in tall chain-link to keep people from wading in and possibly drowning, but there were benches facing the water and they sat together on one, watching the calming, almost hypnotic flow.

"I'm sorry," Ming said finally. "I should have known you couldn't really mean it . . . even though you said you were serious." She glanced at Linnie.

Linnie nodded. "I did say that," she agreed, apologizing. "I was being dramatic. It never occurred to me you'd think I was really serious, though. I can't imagine either of you suddenly planning murders, and I guess I thought you'd automatically know I didn't really mean it."

"It's because . . . that's what I've been wishing," Ming admitted softly. "It's so unfair! I sent out all my college and scholarship applications with number-one class rank on them. I've had to write to everyone and say I'm only number three now, and some of the scholarships were only for valedictorians and salutatorians. It's so humiliating to have to explain."

She sighed and unwrapped the burrito. "I've been writing letters and hating Austin and Adler, wishing they were dead. So when you said let's kill them . . . well. I believed you really meant it because I kind of really wanted it to happen. You must think I'm a real baby, whining about things not being fair."

"Don't be silly." Linnie licked hot sauce off her fingers. "Only what I really had in mind will seem pretty tame now, compared to what you imagined."

Jackson had been busy eating as he listened. He jumped up and put his trash in the barrel, then came back. "Let's hear it," he said.

"It's a game my sister played at a retreat once," Linnie said. "The Dead Game. The way they did it, everyone played and they all knew the rules. We can't play it like that, of course, because we certainly don't want to tell A and A what we're up to. But it's a good starting point."

Ming took small bites of her burrito, listening attentively.

Jackson's watching each bite she takes, Linnie thought. Is he gauging whether there'll be any left for him? "In the real game," she went on, "everyone had an assigned target. And each player was a target, too. So while you were trying to kill your target, someone else was trying to kill you.

"Basically, you had to get your target alone, and then you said, 'You're dead,' or something like that, and then you had to take their target and try to kill that person, too, so the last one left alive was the winner."

She glanced at Jackson. He looked interested. So did Ming.

"What I was thinking," Linnie said, "was that we could do something to A and A. Something that would sting a little, and maybe be symbolic, like . . . oh, I haven't figured that out yet. But they'd know it when they got hit, only they wouldn't know who did it, or why."

"A kind of bloodless vengeance," Jackson muttered. "I like the idea. Only what would we do? How would it actually work?"

"We'd have to do something that had impact," Ming said, frowning.

"What would impact them?" Jackson asked. He stretched his legs out in front of himself, resting his hands on his thighs. "They're not hurting for anything. They've got looks, money, top class rank, huge egos, and successful images."

"That's it!" Ming said, bouncing on the bench. "If we could dent their image we might sting them a little. I have a feeling that's what they value most, anyway. It LOOKS good to graduate first and second. It LOOKS good to go to an Ivy League college. I think they value looks more than anything."

"That's a good point," Linnie said. "What they

value. If we really want to sting someone, it makes sense to figure out what's most important to them and somehow target that." She handed Jackson her crumpled taco wrapper.

He looked at it. "It's empty." He sounded disgusted.

Linnie nodded. He wadded it into a tight ball and tossed it into the bin.

"Austin's hair," Ming said thoughtfully. "He must use a can of hairspray a week on it. It has to look perfect. He probably wouldn't come to school if it didn't look perfect. I wish we could buzz-cut it all off. He'd stay home, and his grades would drop."

"He'd hire a tutor," Linnie said. "Besides, I can't see him sitting still while we cut off his hair. And how would we do it without Austin knowing who'd done it?"

Ming brightened. "His letter jacket!"

"It's certainly important to him." Jackson grinned and stood up, restless. "He makes a big deal out of it, anyway. He's always kind of running his fingers over it, and he hassles anyone who touches it. But what would you do to it?" He took a few steps, came back, glanced toward the river, then at his watch. "I've got track practice pretty soon," he told them.

"I will steal the jacket," Ming announced. "That ought to make an impression on him. He might even get so upset he goes around accusing people and looking like a fool."

She looked over at Linnie, her expression darkening. "Did you know he had the nerve to ask me out?"

Linnie saw Jackson's eyes swing to Ming, his jaw tightening.

Oh! Linnie thought. If I were in a cartoon, light bulbs would be going on above my head. Jackson likes Ming!

"He made it sound like he was doing me a favor," Ming said. "He stood there in his jacket acting like he was granting his attention to a peasant. After what his coming here cost me I could have . . ."

She shook her head, giving a half-laugh. "I almost said I could have killed him," she admitted.

Chapter 4

Linnie, Ming, and Jackson sat at their lunch table the next day, staring across the room at Austin.

"I don't see how you could have done it," Linnie said doubtfully. "He's got it on."

"I feel like a fool," Ming said.

"Are you sure you got the right jacket?" Linnie asked.

"Of course I'm sure! How many prep school letter jackets are there around here? I'm telling you, I took his jacket yesterday and I put it in the woods." Ming glared at Austin. He was sitting sideways to them, obviously wearing the same letter jacket he always wore.

"Tell us what happened," Linnie suggested. "Step by step. Maybe there was another jacket similar to his and you got it by mistake."

Ming rolled her eyes. "There was no mistake. I was going home after we split up. Jackson went to practice, you went back toward the front of the school, and I cut on through the park. I usually go home that way if the sprinklers aren't on."

"Right," Linnie said.

"I went past the stairs and into the woods and then I heard voices murmuring, kind of quiet. I didn't feel like interrupting anyone, so I was going to turn around and go back the other way, but that meant going up all those stairs and I decided I could probably just sneak by whoever was talking because it sounded like . . . well, it sounded like a guy and girl in private conversation. And it was."

She rubbed her forehead. "It was Austin and Brenda. The jacket was behind them on a rock, with their books and stuff. They were too busy kissing to notice me, and besides, I was very quiet. I couldn't believe my luck! I decide to steal Austin's jacket and there it is, right in front of me. It was like a sign. I just grabbed it and kept on going. It was his jacket! I know it was!"

"What did you do with it?" Jackson asked.

"I hung it in that old graveyard," Ming told them, her eyes crinkling as she smiled. "I hung it over a tombstone. It was still there this morning. I checked."

"Well, I guess he found it after you checked, then," Linnie said. "Because he certainly has it on."

"Let's go look," Jackson suggested.

They quickly finished eating and Ming led the way out the back door of the cafeteria, past the huge trash bins, down the steep stairs onto the grassy park grounds, and into the woods. The sun warmed their shoulders until they got into thicker trees. They followed a path, scurrying noises darting ahead of them, then falling silent as squirrels and chipmunks hustled away from the intrusion.

"Over here," Ming said, pointing. "See? That's where I found the jacket. I just picked it up. I didn't even have to stop. I figured they'd go back to school since they both had cars in the lot so I went on this way. I have to admit I was feeling pretty good about the whole thing working out like that. I felt sneaky, but it felt good, like I was finally doing something instead of just giving up."

A slight breeze made the branches creak, and Linnie was suddenly glad it was bright daylight. Their feet scuffled in the layer of old leaves as Ming led them onto a fainter, less well-traveled path. She stopped and pointed.

The clearing ahead was bright, but shadowed in spots. Straight ahead the sun shone on half a dozen ancient tombstones.

"That's fabulous," Linnie said, stepping nearer. "Very artistic."

The tombstone looked as if it were wearing the jacket.

"And that *is* his jacket." Ming sounded almost relieved.

"How long did this take you?" Jackson asked.

"Not very long," Ming said. "The rocks and sticks were all around here. I just had to arrange them." She knelt next to the grave, knelt outside the ring of stones she'd spaced around the mound. "I thought if he went looking for the jacket, it would be nice and spooky for him to find this."

She straightened the rock that was the head, patted the side of the mound and fussed with the sticks she'd laid as bones on top of the grave. "I was very careful to make the bones as realistic as I could. Here's the femur, patella, tibia, fibula . . ."

Linnie shivered. The effect suddenly looked too real. Rocks and sticks, she told herself. That's not really bones. The real bones are six feet under and a hundred years old. "Let's go back," she said. "We saw the jacket. Lunch is almost over."

Ming nodded. She gave the leg bones a final twitch and stood up.

"He's rich," Jackson said as they headed back. "I'll bet he just went out and bought another jacket."

"You can't just go buy a letter jacket," Linnie said. "Especially one from a school in another state."

"I guess if you're rich enough you can do anything, because he's got another jacket on," Jackson pointed out.

"So much for denting his image," Ming said, tossing her hair back. "We didn't even scratch it. I really feel stupid, going to all that effort. I kept imagining his face when he saw the grave and realized it was his jacket. I was hoping he'd have a bunch of people with him and he'd lose his poise in front of them. Instead, I'm the fool."

"You had the right idea," Jackson said, holding a branch out of their way. "We just need to carry it further. There's no point in hitting a target if the target has no idea he's been hit. We should have planned the grave. We should have lured Austin out to see it. Then he'd have felt the hit."

"It's kind of lost its impact, now, since he already has another jacket," Ming pointed out.

They hurried across the grass as the warning bell sounded from above them. From behind them a *ti-ti-ti-ti-whirrrr* sounded and Linnie jumped. "Oh," she said. "The sprinklers. We're going to get wet — unless you want to go back through the park and around the front?"

"We'll just run," Jackson said. "We'll barely get sprinkled."

"Run?" Linnie asked. "Up those steps?" She put a hand on the railing and stared up the steep flight of concrete steps.

"I do it for football training," Jackson said. "Watch." He ran up the stairs, stepping on each stair with first one foot, then the other, as if he were running through staggered tires on an obstacle course.

"I guess I'll be late to pottery if I don't run," Linnie said, laughing as the park sprinkler whirred in their direction, spattering her and Ming as they dashed up the stairs.

At the top, resting briefly, Jackson said, "Listen, Ming. The grave was great. It was our idea that was dumb, not your execution. We should have thought it out better. Let's try again. We'll meet for hamburgers and talk about it. After school."

"And I have someone else to add to the list," Linnie said. "I thought we could make a hit list. But I better run. See you later."

She did run, the *tick-tick-hiss* of the sprinklers

fading as she entered the building. But she was late, anyway. She had to meekly endure the "artists may forget to eat, sleep, and breathe" lecture, but the teacher did admire her vase.

"It's got an intriguing shape," the teacher commented critically. "It's almost a statement. I think it might be one of your better efforts."

Linnie's pleasure was only slightly dimmed when the teacher was just as generous praising Brenda's lump of clay.

That's okay, you're on the list, Linnie thought, winking at Brenda. But Brenda was looking the other way, watching her own reflection in a little pocket mirror she had pulled from her purse, and fussing with her hair.

Chapter 5

"First, it was too easy," Ming said. "And second, it didn't work because it didn't have any effect."

"There needs to be an effect," Linnie agreed. She opened the bag and handed Ming a shake, took the iced tea she'd ordered, and gave the rest to Jackson.

They'd met at the hamburger joint at Jackson's suggestion, carrying their food outside for privacy while they plotted.

"So we know what was wrong with our idea," Jackson said, unwrapping his first burger. "How can we make it right?"

"I've been thinking about that," Ming said. "All games have rules, right? And they have goals. You know when you've won. This is a game. We need rules. Tell us about the real game's rules."

"My sister was at a resort hotel when she played it," Linnie said, idly watching the cars that turned into the lot.

"One of the rules was you had to be alone with your target to kill him, but alone meant that no one else in the group could be within eyesight. Other people from the hotel could be there, but not one of the other group people. And you couldn't use force to get someone alone. Like you couldn't drag your target away from people to get him alone. And you couldn't kill him in his own hotel room, or during the retreat functions."

"So it was actually kind of hard to kill someone," Ming said.

Linnie nodded.

Jackson played imaginary drums on his knees while he chewed his hamburger. "I don't see how that helps us much," he said, taking a drink of water. "All we know so far is we're not stealing any more jackets. And I'm not telling anyone, 'Bang, you're dead.' They'll have to figure it out from what we do. But what are we doing?"

Ming turned to Linnie.

"We need something more than a jacket," Linnie said, thinking. "I liked the idea of something symbolic. And we need it to be more public than the jacket was."

"Something that's more humiliating to the target than to me," Ming said.

"Humiliation is more humiliating if it's public," Jackson announced, drumming it.

"I like the sound of that," Linnie said. "That can be one of our rules. Whatever we do, we have to cause a public humiliation for it to be a hit. Don't forget, I have someone to add to the list."

Jackson unwrapped his last burger. "Who?"

"Brenda," Linnie said. "Because she fakes herself into an A in Studio. The teacher doesn't give very many A's, so Brenda's cheating someone else out of a grade they've actually earned, just by having artistically temperamental fits."

"So there's another rule," Ming pointed out. "The people on the list have to be cheating, somehow, and their cheating has to be keeping the people who earned something from having it."

"Then Karl DeBerg qualifies," Linnie said. "Remember the seventh-grade science fair?"

"I do," Jackson said. "Karl won it with a study of cannonball and bullet trajectories. It was great."

"He won," Linnie said. "But it wasn't really his project. His older sister did it. She was in tenth grade then, which I'd say gave Karl a slight edge over the competition!"

"You took second!" Jackson said. "You should have gotten first place."

Linnie nodded. "First-place winner got their picture in the paper, got out of school to go to the state competition, and won forty dollars. Second place got a ribbon. I still have the ribbon."

"He's on the list." Jackson wrote his name in the air. "We're up to four targets."

"John," Linnie said.

"Stalley?" Ming asked. "Absolutely. John Stalley is the biggest sleaze to ever hit this school. He not only passes on dirt; he makes it up. He threatens to spread rumors about any female who turns him down . . . and then he does, whether she turns him down or not."

Jackson was watching Ming out of the corner of

his eye. "I hope you're not speaking from experience," he said.

Ming looked up, surprised. "Of course I am," she said. "He told me he'd heard I got my grades because I kissed up to the teachers and if I didn't go out with him, he'd send a letter to the school board exposing me."

Jackson's eyebrows lowered.

"I told him to go ahead," Ming went on. "I said the worst they'd do would be to make me take a few tests to see if I knew my work and I could ace any test they could find. I told him he'd be exposed, not me. So he started a bunch of disgusting rumors about me that eventually died down, and all was well again. But he's a sleaze."

Jackson looked even angrier and Linnie wondered how Ming could be missing all the cues. He really likes her, Linnie thought. And she doesn't seem to notice a thing.

"Speaking of rumors," he said finally, "the one about Price is true."

"What rumor?" Linnie asked, rattling the ice in her cup, trying to decide if she was thirsty enough for a refill.

"Let's just say his performance is not all natural," Jackson said.

"I heard he's on steroids," Ming said. "It's true?"

"I never heard that," Linnie said. "Why do you hear everything? I thought I heard everything that went around, but obviously not."

"Sports," Ming said loftily, flexing her arm. "We

athletes are the true source of all knowledge."

"You're not even in track," Linnie said, flicking an ice cube at Ming.

"I am," Jackson said, glancing at his watch. "And I'm due at practice any minute."

"A lot of my basketball and volleyball buddies are on the track team," Ming said. "I still have my sources, even if I'm not active. I hear a lot about Price because people are afraid. If he gets caught, not only do they lose their ace performer, but the coach will be investigated for contributing — which he isn't, but they'll check anyway — and the team will probably get stripped of its past wins and be disqualified from competition this year."

"What I hate is what he's doing to himself," Jackson muttered. He stood up, leaned over the table. "I can't stop him. I keep giving him things to read about how bad steroids are. I don't know if he even reads them. He just tells me to get off his back. I try to talk to him and he goes nuts. He's unpredictable and I'm worried. In a way, I want him to get caught because maybe they'll make him stop. He's killing himself this way. I just hate to see the team go down with him."

"We'll walk you to practice," Linnie offered, jumping up.

Jackson, his natural restlessness erupting, jogged ahead of them for a minute, then returned, almost running in place as he kept pace beside them.

"Price makes an interesting target," Ming said, looking thoughtful.

"He fits the rules," Linnie said. "He profits by

cheating. He's keeping people from winning fairly because he's winning unfairly."

"And he's doing the same thing to himself, too," Ming pointed out. "Which makes him both the victim and the victimizer." She shifted her book bag to her other shoulder. "Is that our list then? Austin, Adler, Brenda, Karl, John, and Price?"

Jackson stopped jogging momentarily. "I want to add two names," he said. "But I don't want to explain why." He flushed. "I guess that's not fair."

"It's okay with me," Ming said. "I trust you. As long as they fit the rules, I'm willing to add them."

"Rafe Gibbons," Jackson said. "I thought he was perfect and he wasn't. And Julie Clay."

He sounds so grim, Linnie thought. It's only a game, right?

Chapter 6

Eight people, Linnie thought.

Austin, Adler, Brenda, Karl, John, Price, Rafe, and Julie.

Eight cheats. Eight fakers. Eight people who got something by cheating someone else out of it.

She programmed the CD player to randomly mix songs from all five CD's she'd chosen, and settled in at the table to study. Her books were strewn around her, a glass of ice and a can of Sprite within reach.

She read the English assignment. *Change this paragraph from passive to active voice.*

Easy, she thought. Cut all the *ing* endings and make them all *ed.*

Instead she scribbled a list of people.

Austin, Adler, Brenda, Karl, John, Price, Rafe, and Julie.

Then she listed the rules they'd worked out before and after Jackson's practice.

— Pick a name from a hat.

*— You have approximately two weeks to do
your hit.*

*— If you can't do it within a reasonable
amount of time, put the name back and let
someone else try.*

— A successful kill is a public humiliation.

*— The more appropriate the humiliation, the
more humiliating and the more public, the
better the kill.*

*— Work alone. No telling whose name you
have. No help from the group, no telling the
game to anyone else. You can get help from
others outside the group, but only if you do
it without letting anything slip about the
game, the purpose, or the group.*

*— After everyone's been hit, we'll vote on the
best kill and treat the winner to something.*

Linnie turned her attention back to the English
assignment. It wasn't as simple as she'd thought.
Changing the endings made the paragraph non-
sense. I think I was thinking of participles or something, she decided. There must be more to passive
voice than I thought. When in doubt, look it up.

But instead of looking in her English book, she
found herself writing a different paragraph.

*My first victim: John. The womanizing
sleaze. What do I know about him? I know
he's eighteen. He's probably going to be a con*

*man when he grows up. He's already a con
man. He looks for weak spots and pushes on
them until you cave in. He's probably dated
every female at Hollander who's good-looking,
popular, or rich. Including me, so I guess I'd
better stretch the list to include every female
who's afraid of being laughed at by good-
looking, popular, or rich kids, too.*

She shuddered, remembering their date. She'd
been flattered when he asked her out. They'd both
been in tenth grade, but unlike John, she wasn't
very self-assured. He'd fed her a few lines, which
she'd believed. She met him as arranged, and he'd
taken her directly to the place everybody called
Beer Can Hill. She'd known, then, exactly what he
had in mind.

I had real-life training in being humiliated even
before that day, she thought, idly X-ing out English
endings. Thanks — I guess — to my sister. She
was an expert at humiliating me. I guess I figured
out pretty early the only way to win was to run
away. That's humiliating, too, because then they
laugh and tell everyone what a coward you are. But
it's less damaging in the long run than staying and
letting them work you over.

Linnie drew dark, heavy lines under John's
name.

You told everyone I didn't know how to kiss, she
thought, drawing a little coffin under his name. You
told them I was so ugly you weren't interested, and
you said I cried because you took me home.

You ruined a whole year of my life.

She drew a skull in the coffin.

Nothing happened. I got out of your car and I walked home. That's what really happened. But nobody would believe me by the time you got done spreading rumors . . . just like you did to Ming and all the others.

It's our turn to get back at you. Victim's revenge. I have to think of a fitting punishment. I owe it to all of them — all of your victims. What if . . .

Smiling, she drew little rocks around the coffin, like Ming had put around the grave. She felt like an avenging angel.

She had an idea.

Something public.

And very humiliating.

"I need a small microphone," Linnie explained to the clerk. She'd left her unfinished English homework and had driven twenty miles to the next town, to a different mall from the one she usually went to. She hadn't seen anyone she knew.

"The recorder has to be small, too, but the microphone can't be any bigger than a quarter or so. We just have small writing surfaces in the lecture hall, and my books and things take up most of the space. I can't set up a microphone and still have room to take notes. And I sit in the back of the hall. It has to be a good microphone."

"We've got some excellent microphones," the clerk assured her. "I'm afraid they're kind of expensive."

"If I flunk, I lose my scholarship," Linnie said. "The microphone will be cheap compared to a semester of college!"

"I see." The clerk looked sympathetic. "If you don't want to worry about setting the mike up, you might want to consider a wireless. You could pin it on your collar, or even stick it on the professor's desk and still pick up the whole lecture from your desk in the back of the room. You don't even have to take the tape recorder out of your book bag, especially this model. It's particularly designed to be sensitive to the human voice."

Perfect, Linnie thought.

The recorder and microphone cost plenty, but she bought them, taking them home and playing with them all evening until she was fairly confident of their range and sensitivities. She'd been assistant to the assistant sound-and-lighting-control person for the Thespian Society — working the control panel for sound and lights for the school plays for a whole year — so she already had a basic understanding of distance, clarity, and tonal quality when recording music and the human voice.

She found the miniature system satisfactory, able to pick up music from the stereo from twenty feet or more with no distortion.

Perfect, Linnie thought again. I'm now prepared to commit the perfect "murder."

Chapter 7

Ming finished her homework quickly and neatly.

Her parents were at meetings, but they'd brought home a pizza, leaving it in the fridge with a note.

Enjoy. Left the Mazda if you need a car. Back late. Hugs and kisses.

She wondered how many X's and O's they would have written if they were still signing with X's and O's. Kisses and hugs, she thought, folding the note. X's for kisses, O's for hugs. I used to get five each when I was little. Unless I'd done something special. Then I'd get eight. And an exclamation point. I used to put the note under my pillow at night to help me get to sleep.

She put two pieces of pizza on a plate and stuck it in the microwave. When it buzzed, she took the plate to the table, stacked her books, got milk, a napkin, and a fork.

While she ate, she thought about Rafe, the name she'd drawn.

Jackson only said he thought Rafe was perfect and he wasn't. What does that mean? He sounded pretty grim, so Rafe must have done something pretty bad. But what kind of thing?

She cut a bite of pizza off with her fork. John would be easy. I wish I'd drawn his name. I know what he does, so I'd know how to humiliate him — make him look like the lying, rumor-spreading creep he is. What a strange idea, that I could humiliate someone by showing the world what he actually is. That's ironic. Would it work with everyone? Is that the key? Not really, I guess. Obviously exposure is only humiliating if a person is ashamed or embarrassed by what he is.

When she finished eating she drank her milk, then rinsed her dishes and put them in the dishwasher. She got out a piece of paper.

How can I expose Rafe for what he really is when I don't know what he really is?

She stared at the blank paper for a while, then wandered around the house, looking for inspiration. In the den, she turned the TV on, then back off, looked through their collection of movies, thumbed through the tapes and CD's.

Wait a minute, movies! Bad guys and problems and resolutions. There may be an idea there.

She thought back over her favorite movies, then laughed at herself, realizing she mostly watched high-action adventure shows where the hero was always in great physical danger, performing impossible feats by the end of the show.

I'm afraid my problem isn't that dramatic, she decided, recalling some of her favorite fight scenes, fiery crashes, and incredible rescues. When I was little I used to reenact the good parts over and over, she remembered. I'd practice karate on trees, I'd wrestle anybody who'd come close enough to challenge . . . what a little terror I was. Maybe I should forget movies and try something less dramatic. I go to school. I should be able to think of something!

She headed back to the kitchen, and the blank piece of paper, which she stared at again.

Darn it! I have a very simple problem here and I don't have the faintest idea how to solve it. Why don't they teach us anything practical in school?

Chapter 8

Jackson drummed on his knees, staring at the name *Brenda.*

Brenda, Brenda, he thought. Fluffy hairdo. Lots of makeup. Fancy clothes. One of those bouncy types — always talking and flirting. Brenda who smashes pots in Studio Art class. Brenda, who has artistic fits to impress the teacher.

Jackson stood up and wandered into the kitchen to check for lemonade. The beasts — his half brothers, ages five and three and a half — were setting up a last-ditch effort to escape bedtime.

"But I'm hungry!"

"I didn't get no dessert!"

"Any dessert," Jackson told the little one, patting his head.

"You're not so smart," Wesley, the five-year-old, told Jackson. "Daddy said so."

"Hush," his mother said, giving Jackson an apologetic and harried glance.

I'm no genius, Jackson agreed silently. He poured the lemonade, told the beast-children good night, and escaped back to his room, closing his door on their protests.

No great genius, no great athlete. Not even a great son, stepson, or stepbrother.

He turned his radio on, keeping the sound low.

Okay, so I'm not great. I can live with that.

Still, remembering the harried look in his mother's eyes, he sighed. I'm not helpful. I could at least be helpful.

Sighing again he went back to the kitchen and swooped up the beasts — one in each arm. The boys shrieked happily, pounding on his shoulders.

"Muscles!" Wesley crowed. "Carry us up!"

"Up!" the little one echoed.

"They've had their baths and brushed their teeth," his mother said, smiling gratefully. "It just remains to get them in bed and keep them there long enough to fall asleep."

Jackson carried the squirming boys up the stairs, bouncing on each step. He plunked them in the wrong beds, to their delight, and would only let them switch back when they promised to hug tight to their teddy bears and not let them loose till morning.

That'll keep their hands occupied, he thought.

"Story!" Wesley demanded.

Jackson thought for a moment, then told them a story about Brenda, a pretend person who thought she was real and spent all day bothering people so they would notice her.

Chapter 9

"So how goes the hunt?" Jackson asked. He'd just come through the line but his tray was nearly empty.

"Why aren't you eating?" Linnie asked. "Don't you like the school's burritos?"

"I like everything if it's food," Jackson informed her. "I ate my burrito already."

"Between the kitchen and the table?" Linnie shook her head. "How are things going for you?"

Jackson shrugged. "I'm not sure. The only thing I'm sure of is that things seem very different lately. There's a new slant on the world, and on the way I see things."

"I'll say!" Linnie agreed. "I keep finding myself thinking about and noticing all kinds of different things, and I zone out on the stuff I'm supposed to be doing."

"Me, too," Ming said, joining them at the table. "I've never had to remind myself to pay attention in class before. It's kind of fun being an airhead."

She sliced her burrito in half and gave half to Jackson.

"I've got a plan of attack!" Linnie announced, leaning forward, keeping her voice low. "I'm so excited! Did you notice anything different about me today?"

Jackson and Ming both looked at her carefully, finally shaking their heads.

"Good!" Linnie said smugly. "Then it's working."

"I have a fairly good idea what I'm going to do," Ming told them. "It kind of depends on the lunch menu, but they all look reasonably good."

Jackson raised an eyebrow.

"No fair asking questions," Linnie reminded him.

"I didn't say a word."

"You looked like you were going to."

Ming smiled. "I feel like a crook," she said. "Planning a job. A bank job, maybe. It's so much fun to walk around knowing I get to murder someone and they don't know anything about it!"

"Well, I haven't got a plan of attack," Jackson admitted. "I'm having a terrible time coming up with an idea. But it is fun stalking the victim. It's like on TV where the bad guy stakes out a place and learns the victim's habits, like what time she's due home and when and where she shops. Maybe I'll be a detective after I graduate."

"You'll have to learn how to plan attacks, then," Ming said. "And how to be more discreet. You just said 'she,' so now we can guess which names you didn't draw."

"Oops. Maybe I was just using *she* the way most people use *he*."

"Maybe." Ming grinned. "But since you're having so much fun stalking, I'm going to guess it's a she."

"Um . . . excuse me. Jackson, do you still want this? It's cold now. Sorry."

Jackson smiled at the girl who had interrupted them. "Cold burritos are my favorite," he said. "Thank you very much."

When the girl was gone, Linnie said, "I wanted to mention that since we're all kind of busy researching our new project, maybe we should arrange to meet regularly outside of school or something."

Ming nodded. "I was going to bring that up, myself. I'll need to be absent during lunch one of these days. Well, not absent from school, just absent from our group. And it might look better if I joined other tables at lunch between now and then so it's not so obvious."

"Gotcha," Jackson said, tapping on the tabletop. "How about we meet Mondays after track practice — say five? At the field? I have to get home pretty quick after practice but let's try it. If it doesn't give us enough time we can work something else out."

And I need to find the chink in Brenda's armor, he told himself. Linnie and Ming both have plans of attack laid out and I haven't the foggiest idea how I'm going to do Brenda in.

Chapter 10

The next week, on Tuesday, Ming examined her "R-Notes."

Rafe's last class before lunch — Chemistry.
East wing. Always arrives at IN door: 11:59.
Brings lunch from home. Eats with: blond guy
in leather jacket and dark-haired guy, very
short hair.

She'd arranged the information in graph form, with M-T-W-Th-F along the side, and headings across the top.

This is what I'm good at, she thought, eyeing her graph. Gathering, compiling, organizing, and remembering information. I can write reports, remember facts, understand the relationship of one table of data to another.

But DO something with it?

I'm afraid.

Rafe will walk through that door within the next five minutes, paper bag in his jacket pocket, two friends — one on either side — and he'll walk directly to that table there. One friend will sit with him, the other will go buy milk for everyone.

She laughed, almost choking on the grape she'd been chewing.

Milk! she thought. If he's the bad guy, it doesn't seem right for him to be drinking milk! Somehow that makes him seem more like a little kid. Little kids don't have egos like his, though. And little kids act real.

She was standing near the OUT door, watching the hall, holding her tray. Fruit cup, spaghetti, buttered bread, corn, milk.

She'd picked the grapes out of the fruit cup, nibbling nervously while she waited, making herself watch for Rafe and not try to locate Jackson or Linnie, not try to catch their attention or see if they were watching her.

She waited until 12:07, then gave up, sitting with a crowd from her Math Analysis class, watching the door.

Rafe never came.

That really messes up my graph, Ming thought. Now I'll have to redo it and add some new headings.

Linnie paused, a few feet behind John.

Initially she'd been worried about picking up the hall noise and voices other than John's. But it seemed that whenever John Stalley moved in, everyone else got quiet. The tapes had been excellent so far.

"So, baby." John made the words last a long time,

as if he enjoyed the sound of them. "How's things?"

The poor sophomore, Linnie thought. She's overwhelmed. She can only smile adoringly. Poor baby! She's going to wish she'd never met this creep. And the sad thing is, she probably knows that already!

"You sure you can get out tonight?" John asked.

The girl nodded eagerly, then frowned. "I thought . . . I heard Brenda . . . she says you've got a date with her."

"She'll wait," John said. "They all wait. Tonight it's you I want."

He leaned closer to the girl, running his left hand down her right arm, ending at her fingers. He grasped her hand. "Tonight?"

"Oh, yes!" she said. "I can get out. I'll tell them I have a baby-sitting job."

Beautiful! Linnie thought. Perfect!

Doesn't she ever get tired of shopping? Jackson wondered, leaning against the wall just outside the store where Brenda was selecting items to look at and try on. Suddenly he stiffened. Blinked.

Did I see that? I think I did. Yes, I did. I saw it.

Gotcha! he thought. Oh baby, I found the chink in your armor!

How can I use it?

Chapter 11

Wednesday, Ming waited, watching through the OUT door to see if Rafe passed by.

When he did, at 11:59, she could feel her muscles tense, her mouth go dry.

She took a step, felt her knees trembling.

Rafe turned right, instead of left, standing in the hot lunch line.

With a mixture of relief and disappointment, Ming joined the Classics Discussion group, trying to immerse herself in the argument about Silas Marner.

I'm a coward, Ming thought. I was so relieved that he went the other way! He has to turn this way or else I'd have had to crowd around all those tables to get near him. He ruined my plan and I'm kind of glad, but I'm a coward because I'm not doing anything. I'm using the Dead Game as an excuse to feel better about Austin and Adler, but I'm not getting a hit on Rafe, either.

* * *

Thursday Rafe showed up at 12:09, a girl clinging tightly to his arm. While Ming hesitated, Rafe and the girl sat at a table.

I'm running out of time, Ming thought. The two weeks is up pretty soon. I have to be ready for these changes. I have to be more flexible. Just because he's a few minutes later, or turns the wrong way, or has another person with him doesn't mean I couldn't do it anyway. I'm looking for excuses.

Maybe tomorrow. Maybe Friday will be my day.

Chapter 12

"Now I've been with girls and I've been with women," John said. He'd gone into what Linnie called his confidentially-speaking-doesn't-my-deodorant-smell-good pose, leaning on the girl's locker with one arm extended in front of her, and one arm draped loosely over her shoulders.

"It's not the age that makes a woman, you understand. It's the attitude."

The girl — another sophomore — looked unblinkingly into his face.

Mesmerized by the sheer force of his personality, no doubt, Linnie thought.

"Now, Mary Ann . . . you know Mary Ann, don't you?"

The girl nodded.

"Mary Ann, well, she's a real sweet little girl. There's that word, *girl*. I thought . . . well, you know. She told me she loved me so I thought . . . well. She's just too young. She'll grow up one of these days. Now, you. You're different. I can tell. Are you sure you can get out tonight? Maybe your folks won't let you out, even if it is Friday. Maybe you have to stay home Friday nights?"

"I'll get out. I'll meet you. Eight o'clock, right?"

He doesn't even change his lines, Linnie thought, absently patting her book pack. I've heard this a dozen times already.

"I could go to the party with you," the girl said hopefully.

"Oh, we'll see," John said. "Who knows what'll develop by then."

I know what will develop by then, Linnie thought. Nothing. It's Brenda's party. No way is he going to show up with a sophomore! Especially since I happen to know Brenda invited him as her date.

Wait! The party! Linnie thought. I have enough! I can edit tapes after school, make my final tape, show up at the party, and make sure it gets played. Almost everyone who'll be there is mentioned on one of my tapes — Brenda especially. And it's HER party!

This is going to be good!

Chapter 13

Jackson watched Brenda all day Friday.

The girl is a total fake, he thought. She hasn't got a real feeling, emotion, opinion, or action in her entire being.

He watched her invite people to her party, then turn around a minute later and say, "Oh, I'm sorry. I forgot you didn't make the cheerleading squad. Well, never mind about the party. You wouldn't feel comfortable there, I'm sure." She shrugged apologetically. "Oops."

Or, "You didn't get accepted at Yale, after all," or "I forgot you can't dance."

Why? Jackson wondered, shaking his head. Why do people hurt each other like that? She has to know what she's doing.

Brenda noticed Jackson eventually and turned her charm on him.

"Football," she said definitely. "I know I've seen you on the field with a football. It's Jackson, isn't it?"

"I think I heard someone say that," Jackson said, mentally checking his defenses.

"Such a . . . different name. Wherever did your parents find it?"

"In the Bible," Jackson said solemnly.

Her eyes widened. "Oh! A Bible name. How special."

"Not so special," Jackson said. "Lots of names are in the Bible. Matthew, Mark, Luke, John, Brenda."

"You're kidding!"

"Probably," Jackson agreed.

"You know I'm having a party tonight," Brenda said, leaning toward him.

"No!"

She nodded. "And I'd like you to come."

"Oh, I couldn't." Jackson grinned shyly, leaning forward, as if in response to her. "I have to wash my hair." He walked off quickly before Brenda could say anything back. He had to bite his lip to keep from laughing.

He caught quite a few admiring glances and knew two things — he'd just made himself quite a few friends, and he'd just made himself one ruthless enemy.

It's okay, he thought. Because I've got her.

Chapter 14

Friday at lunch, Ming waited.

The menu was spicy barbecued beef on a bun, french fries, Jell-O, and milk.

She'd loaded her fries with a mound of ketchup, had opened her milk carton. The sandwich was open face, both sides covered with sauce and thin slices of meat. The Jell-O quivered in response to the shaking of her knees.

She saw Rafe through the OUT door, saw him and his two friends. Saw the end of the paper lunch bag in his pocket. No girl.

For Jackson, she thought, forcing herself to step forward, to walk the imaginary line she'd drawn that would intersect Rafe's path.

One step. Two.

For Jackson and all the other people you hurt.

Three steps.

Six.

Ming managed to bump Rafe perfectly. His elbow knocked the tray from her hands. Barbecued beef slid down the front of his shirt, leaving brownish-red smears. Great slops of milk, ketchup, and Jell-O went flying.

Rafe wiped at his shirt, muttering angrily. He took a step back as Ming's tray hit the floor.

Then the people behind him surged forward and Rafe fell forward. Off balance, his arms flew out.

Ming had been pushed backward in the odd surge, but she reached out automatically to grab at Rafe's arm, to try to steady him.

This isn't part of the plan, she had time to think.

Then, rapid-fire, Rafe — still off balance and flailing for a handhold — stepped in Ming's tray, and propelled by the people behind him, who were also falling, he went sliding and tumbling into a crowd of people. Several of them held trays; some tripped over Rafe, some dropped trays on him. It seemed like Rafe fell in silence, in single-frame slow motion.

The startled yells hit Ming like a fist as sound and movement erupted.

Ming tried to push forward to the pile of fallen trays and people. Rafe was on the bottom. She'd seen the whole thing, and it played in reverse as the pile began to undo itself, revealing a silent, unmoving Rafe, on the floor, smeared with food.

Ming had almost reached him when the first teacher finally took over, ordering people to sit at a table. NOW!

What have I done?

Ming's chest hurt, her knees threatened to collapse, her teeth were clenched so tightly that the muscles in her jaw quivered. She pushed forward.

51

The crowd began to thin as people found chairs and got out of the way. A lot of people were spattered with food. A couple were limping. Only Rafe was lying still, uncomplaining, unmoving.

He . . . I saw . . . someone kicked him in the head, Ming thought. And then his neck snapped back. He looked . . . shocked.

She wiped her eyes, but the scene kept replaying, forward this time, from the beginning.

Someone landed on him, hard. I saw knees hit him in the chest . . . his head snapped back from the kick . . . and then someone fell right across his back. What happened to his face? People were falling all over him.

What have I done?

"You! Miss!"

Dumbly Ming realized the teacher was talking to her.

"Go to the office. We need an ambulance. Can you manage?"

Ming nodded.

"Fast!"

The cafeteria had cleared out enough so Ming could run.

I didn't mean for that to happen.

She gave her message at the office, then ran back to the cafeteria where she sat, tears running down her face, until the ambulance arrived and a pale, silent, motionless Rafe was taken off on a stretcher.

Chapter 15

We're at the theater tonight. We knew you'd have plans since it's Friday. Left you the Mazda. Home by 1:30. Hugs and kisses.

The note was taped to a Chinese takeout dinner in neat, white boxes with metal handles, which meant Ming had to dump the food on a plate before she could microwave it.

Her parents worked in the city, commuting an hour each way. They wanted their daughter to grow up in the suburbs, but they never spent any time there, themselves. They left the house before Ming got up, and like true bankers, got to work by six A.M., brought something home for her for dinner around three-thirty, then went back into the city almost every night for dinner, the theater, more work, shopping, or whatever. They slept most of the weekend to make up for their frantic schedules. Ming wondered why they didn't just move into the city. Maybe they would after Ming went away to college.

She tried to remember when she'd last seen her parents — actually seen them or talked to them for more than five minutes.

She decided it had been almost six years ago at her twelfth birthday party, but she knew she was exaggerating, trying to divert her thoughts from the lunchroom.

At first it worked just right, she thought. Rafe got ketchup and barbecue sauce on his jacket. He looked disgusted. He looked messy. That was perfect.

Then, that surge of people.

What happened?

The phone rang. It was Linnie.

"What happened?" Linnie asked.

"I don't know." She doesn't know I picked his name, Ming thought. But she can guess, I suppose.

"I heard there was a riot in the lunchroom and Rafe got beat up by Sheila's boyfriend because he'd been flirting with her."

Ming sighed. I wish, she thought. "No riot. It was . . . an accident."

"Oh. That's not as interesting."

"I suppose not." Ming wanted to explain her part in the accident. She also didn't want to explain it. I'll have to tell sooner or later, she thought. And I might feel better. But not yet. I can't talk about it yet.

"Are you going to Brenda's party?" Linnie asked.

"She invited me," Ming said. "But I'm not particularly interested."

"I think you should come," Linnie said. "And I

have a very good reason, which I don't want to go into right now. I have the car. Will you go with me?"

I'm not exactly in a party mood, Ming thought. But then, I'm not in the mood to stay home alone, either. "Thanks," she said. "Give me a half hour to get ready."

Ming and Linnie wandered through Brenda's house and yard, then wound up in the shadows alongside the house, watching the party develop around them.

Brenda had a huge backyard, with large bushes and trees, benches, outdoor lights, and a sound system plugged in outside. The food was indoors, the drinks on the deck, and people went from the yard to the deck, into the house, and back out in a constant stream.

Brenda kept checking her watch and looking annoyed.

Your precious John, Linnie wanted to tell her, is out with a tenth-grader. And I'm just as eager as you are for him to get here. Then I'll play my tape and go home.

Actually, he ought to be here pretty soon, she decided, reaching into her purse.

Brenda turned off her look of annoyance when Austin stopped by to talk to her, but as soon as he left, she frowned again.

Linnie couldn't feel the tape. She rummaged around in her purse, feeling again.

"Why do you keep doing that?" Ming asked. "Do

you need something? I have Tylenol. I have tissues."

"I need something, all right," Linnie muttered. "And I know I put it in here."

"Look, there's Jackson." Ming waved. Jackson joined them, hugging them both. Surprised, Ming hugged him back quickly. I needed that, she thought.

"It's so nice to be around *real* people," Jackson said. "You can't imagine!" He pointed at the groups of people scattered across the lawn. "Do you realize the fake-cheat-fraud ratio out there? I'll give you a hint. Brenda invited them."

"She invited me," Ming told him, half smiling.

"You've got status," Jackson said. "You are Most Likely to Succeed, Hollander High's success story — all in capital letters."

"Number three," Ming said.

Jackson grabbed her by the forearms. "Don't DO that!" he said. "Nobody's counting. Nobody who matters, anyway. You've got everything in front of you — engineering school, medical school, anything you want, no matter which number anyone gives you. Don't fall into that number trap. You're good!"

Startled and grateful, Ming tried to think of a response. She felt short of breath, and drew in air, trying to fill her lungs.

"I can't believe this!" Linnie said. "I know I put it in here, but I can't find it!"

"What?" Ming asked.

"Oh . . . something. I came here tonight to do something and I can't find it."

She has a hit planned for the party, Ming thought. Who? Brenda? But almost everyone else on the list is here, too. It could be any one of them, I guess.

The thought of a hit reminded her of Rafe, slipping slow-motion, the kick to his head, the legs twisted, people thudding on him as they fell, the head snapping back too fast and too far.

"Do you know how Rafe's doing?" Ming asked Jackson.

"It's kind of weird," Jackson said. "I can't believe he could get hurt like that in the lunchroom. I heard all kinds of things — he got hit in the chest and the doctors are worried that he might have bruised his heart, he's in a coma, his brain is bruised, he has a concussion — you name it, I've heard it. I don't know what to believe."

Ming felt suddenly smaller as if she'd contracted inward upon herself. It's bad, she thought. I really hurt him.

"I can't believe this!" Linnie said. She knelt down in the arc of light from the back porch and dumped her purse upside down. "What could have happened to it? Did I leave my purse unattended somewhere? Yes, darn it. I did. I left it in the kitchen while I got food and stuff . . . how stupid can I get?"

"What is going on?" Jackson asked her.

Linnie replaced her wallet, bottle of pain reliever, keys, coins, notebook, receipts, gum. "It's gone. Someone took it."

"Took what?" Jackson asked.

Linnie looked both horrified and excited. "Took

my hit," she said. "I was going to do my kill tonight and it's gone. But why would someone take a tape from my purse?"

"A tape?" Ming asked.

"Yeah. Like a tape-recorder-type tape."

"Maybe someone thought it was music," Ming suggested. "Maybe you dropped it."

"Oohhh!" Linnie moaned. "Look, there's John. There's Brenda. Everybody's here! And my tape's gone."

"I knew it would be a very dramatic evening," Jackson said, nodding. "That's why I came, anyway — despite the fact that Brenda invited me."

Chapter 16

Monday morning in homeroom, at precisely 7:42 —
as it did every school morning — the PA system
clicked on.

"Good morning," the principal's voice said. "This
is Monday, April sixth. There are forty-one days of
school left, thirty-six days for seniors. The an-
nouncements this morning are . . ."

The sound of paper rustling, then a click.

"I've been with girls, and I've been with women."

The voice permeated the school. The principal
could no longer be heard. Linnie sat up straight,
her eyes wide.

*"It's not the age that makes a woman, you un-
derstand. It's the attitude."* The voice was clear,
seductively conversational.

My tape! Linnie thought. That's my tape!

*"Brenda now. She's a senior, but she's a baby. I
know fourteen-year-olds who are more mature . . .*

"They'll wait. They all wait . . .

*"Oh, no, Brenda, there's no one else. Just
you . . .*

"Baby . . . baby . . . baby."

I don't believe this! Jackson thought. Is this Linnie's hit? It's got to be. If it is, she just won. This is spectacular!

"She told me she loved me. I thought . . . well, you know . . . you know. I've been with girls and I've been with women — women — women."

Linnie glanced from side to side, eyeing people, checking their reactions, hoping her own guilty knowledge didn't show. Heads had gone up in attention, faces lit with recognition. A few girls giggled. The guys looked gleeful.

"It's John Stalley!" someone said, and everyone broke up laughing.

"Who did this?"

Once the question had been asked, Linnie was sure everyone was looking at her. She wanted to shrink in her seat, but she was afraid to do anything that might draw attention to her.

"I wonder why they're letting it play?"

"The principal probably wants to hear the lines."

"Brenda's a baby," the tape continued. *"She's not that good-looking, either. She's a baby. Not like you. Not like you. You. You."*

I knew it was a good tape, Linnie thought, listening to the hoots around her.

The homeroom teacher had seemed as startled and amused as the students, but he finally stood. "Keep yourselves out of trouble," he told the class. "I'll bet someone tapped into the system and the front office can't turn it off. As entertaining as this may be for the school, I guess it's my civic duty to help stop it."

When he opened the door to the hall, Linnie could hear hooting and laughter from all over the school.

The tape played on, with a new voice saying, *"I can get out. I'll tell them I'm baby-sitting."* A series of different voices followed, *"I'm sure I can get out. I'll find a way. I love you, John."*

I'm not half bad at editing, Linnie thought smugly. This is better than I realized. It shows him perfectly.

"I should copy down some of these lines," a guy behind Linnie said dryly. "They obviously worked for John."

"I don't think they'll work after today," someone else told him.

The tape played for another few minutes and then the PA system clicked, popped, gave one shrill shriek, and went dead.

The groans from students resounded through the halls.

Linnie sighed.

"Anybody want to take any bets on how soon John gets another date?" someone asked, grinning.

The school buzzed with laughter and comments the rest of the day. Linnie heard that John had been seen at school that morning before homeroom, but no one had seen him since.

She had no way of knowing whether he'd heard the tape, since he hadn't been in his homeroom class, but as Tuesday and Wednesday went by with no sight of him, she guessed that he had.

I guess my tape worked better here than it would have at the party, she decided. If it was in the hands of fate, the fates couldn't have done a better job. I wonder if I'll ever get it back, though.

Rumors had flown throughout school. Linnie heard that John had left town, that he was hiding out in his basement with the twenty-six girls who'd been absent that Monday — making them the only ones who hadn't heard the tape. She heard he'd developed laryngitis trying to plead his case with Brenda.

By Wednesday afternoon she'd heard that someone had rigged a timer to the tape player in the auditorium, then had run a wire from the tape player to the master panel, bypassing the office and tapping into the PA system, there.

Rumors flew, too, about who was responsible, but since the rumor changed minute by minute, Linnie figured no one really knew who had done it, and whoever really had done it wasn't stepping forward to claim credit.

Chapter 17

"Thank you," Ming said quietly, hanging up the phone. She turned away from the booth, turned out of the phone alcove, and headed upstairs to class.

Thank you for nothing, she thought, nodding automatically at the people who greeted her. What does it mean, no change? What was he like before? What condition is it he hasn't changed from? How is he doing? Will he be okay? I know I'm not family, but why can't they tell me anything? It can't be good that he's in intensive care. Maybe that rumor was true, then. He's in a coma. Maybe he's going to die.

She almost walked into the wall instead of into class, mumbled a startled, "Thanks," at the person who grabbed her arm and aimed her at the doorway.

If he dies, I'm a killer. That's a whole lot worse than losing scholarships and being number three! That's a whole new level of categories — murderer, killer, criminal.

I don't want him to die!

For the first time in her life Ming did not have

the answer when the teacher called on her.

She looked vaguely at the board, not even certain which class she was in.

"Are you okay?" her teacher asked. "Maybe you should go to the nurse's office."

Ming felt tears well up in her eyes, slide down her cheek. She didn't know if she was crying for Rafe or because the teacher didn't understand.

What if he dies?

What good can the nurse do for that?

What if he lives, but he has brain damage and has to be fed and can't even say his name anymore? I'll have to go to nursing school instead of engineering school so I can take care of him. I'll have to take care of him. It's my fault!

She saw again the surge of people, surging forward almost as if they'd been suddenly pushed from behind, falling on Rafe . . . saw the foot as someone stumbled, kicking him in the head, saw his head snap back, saw the pile collapse on him in a mess of barbecued beef and Jell-O and bright red that was not ketchup.

The school nurse sent her home and Ming covered a sheet of paper with X's and O's, put it under her pillow and finally fell asleep, crying.

Chapter 18

On Wednesday, Jackson's plan was ready to be put into action. He slid a folder into his backpack, feeling smug. I'm no great artist, he thought, but I did okay.

Now for the fireworks. Whenever the situation is ripe.

He was so pleased he called hello to people he barely recognized, did his tire-obstacle step up the stairs, and raised his hand in class.

He was disappointed when he saw Brenda at lunch. Conditions weren't ripe.

He was doubly disappointed that he didn't see Ming, but since they'd discussed needing time at lunch to plan and arrange hits, he figured she was busy. But he didn't see her in the halls, either. After asking around, he finally discovered she'd gone home sick. His fabulous mood evaporated.

People get sick, he told himself, trying to concentrate in his afternoon classes. It's no big deal. And it's not like she's your girlfriend or anything. She's just a friend. And co-hitperson.

At that thought he brightened, thinking of the hit on John. That had been fabulous. He hoped his hit went over as well. He wondered what Ming had planned. Ming.

It isn't like her to go home sick, he thought.

He had Phys Ed last hour, and hurried to the gym, looking for the teacher — who was also his track coach. "I'm skipping Phys Ed so I can make practice," Jackson said.

The coach eyed him for thirty solid seconds, his eyes measuring, weighing.

"You have forty-five minutes after school, before practice."

"I don't know if that'll be enough." Jackson waited patiently, keeping his expression determined. He knew the coach was weighing the situation. Should he conspire to allow Jackson an unreported absence, or make him come to class knowing he would then miss practice?

"I understand you will be unavoidably detained for Phys Ed last hour," the coach finally said. "Knowing that in advance, I will not mark you absent. This time."

"Thanks," Jackson said, meaning it.

"Good time last week on the fifty meter," the coach said. "But your kick wasn't its best. Could do better."

"Gotcha." Jackson understood. He'd have to work at bettering his time in the fifty meter in trade for skipping class.

He jogged slowly to Ming's, using the run as a warmup for practice. He rang her doorbell, waited.

He knocked on the door. He rang again, worrying now. What if she'd been too sick to make it home? What if she was lying in the shrubbery somewhere between school and her house? What if she'd cut through the woods and had fallen somewhere off the path? How would he ever find her?

The door opened.

She's been crying, Jackson thought. Her eyes were swollen, her face pale. "What's the matter?" he asked.

Ming blinked hard. "Rafe," she said.

Oh, no! Jackson thought. She's in love with Rafe! He's hurt and she's worried about him.

Without planning it, or even quite knowing how it happened, Jackson found himself hugging Ming, comforting her in her doorway, patting her back, and murmuring, "It's okay. He'll be all right."

"It's my fault," Ming said, sniffing back sobs. She leaned into him, hugging him back.

"It's not your fault. Everyone says he knocked the tray out of your hands." Jackson felt a sweet warmth filling his arms, running into his chest. He remembered hugging his little brothers, how warm and clean-smelling they were after their bath.

This is better, he thought, his arms tightening. This is as nice as it gets.

Ming pulled free, and embarrassed, Jackson dropped his arms. She's smart, he thought. I'm not. There is the whole story in four words. She's-smart-I'm-not. Besides, it looks like she's in love with Rafe.

"Please come in," Ming said formally. "It was

nice of you to come. Would you like a soft drink or something?"

"Water," Jackson said automatically. "I've got track practice later. I have to run faster. Kick better. I'd better stick to water."

"Ice?" Ming asked. "Please sit down." She pointed to the couch.

"No ice, thank you," Jackson said, sinking onto the surprisingly comfortable, modern-looking sofa. He looked around the room while Ming went after water. The house was about as opposite from his as it was possible for a house to get.

There was no clutter at all. No shoes, balls, books, half-eaten sandwiches, crumpled lunch bags, Nintendo games, stray dishes, game pieces, sweatshirts, or forgotten race cars. No remote controls waiting to be reunited with vehicles, no Lego pieces, no crayons. Nothing in the living room was out of place.

The two couches faced each other like enemies, trying to be polite for the sake of the formal flower arrangement, the dramatic, knotted drapes, the framed artwork on the walls.

It was a formal room, looking unused and unfriendly, as if people themselves would clutter it . . . a room to look at, not to use.

No one fidgets in here, he thought, smiling thanks as Ming handed him a glass of cool water, no ice.

"What are you doing out of school?" Ming asked. "It's early."

"You went home sick," Jackson blurted out, then wished he could stuff the words back into his mouth and try again.

Ming smiled, but it was a formal, polite half-smile that crumpled as he watched.

Jackson looked around desperately for a coaster. It was obvious that no one actually put a glass down on these tables — not without a protective barrier. Finally he put the glass on the hearth and stood to face Ming.

"Let's walk," he suggested, almost running to the door and pushing it open. "Come on. You need some exercise."

You idiot! he told himself. She needs exercise? That's a great line. Great. Try to do something right!

"Okay," Ming said obediently. She stepped out onto the porch. "I killed him, you know."

"Rafe? He's not dead."

"He will be." Ming set off at a brisk pace, glancing back at Jackson. "It's only a matter of time."

"But he's doing better!" Jackson said, catching up to her, taking her arm.

"How do you know? No one will tell me anything. I know he's in intensive care and I hear all the rumors, but no one tells me when I call the hospital."

"Our families are friends," Jackson said. "I know his mom. Rafe and I used to be friends. I hear every day how he's doing. He's supposed to get his own room tomorrow."

Ming stood in front of him, looking as if she

wanted to believe him, but couldn't. Abruptly she sat on the curb and wrapped her arms around her legs. "No one would say," she said. "No change. Intensive care. And I did it. It was my hit, Jackson. I put him in the hospital."

"Oh, no," Jackson said softly.

"I just wanted him to look ridiculous!" Ming wailed. "I planned and planned it. It was such a messy lunch. I opened my milk carton and everything. I thought . . . I just wanted him to slip and get messy and look dumb. I didn't want him hurt, not even a little!"

Jackson found his arms around her again, hoping that maybe she wasn't in love with Rafe after all. Quickly he turned his thoughts to fifty-meter dashes and getting his kick right. It was safer.

"It's not your fault," he whispered, slowly dropping his arms. "I nominated him, remember? If it's anyone's fault, it's mine. See, he was perfect. At least, I thought he was. He was a good athlete and a good friend and he could really run. He was the reason the track team took third place at state my sophomore year. He was good."

Jackson paused, swallowed, remembering. "Then he dropped out of track. He just dropped out. Quit the team. He wouldn't talk to me about it or listen or anything. My junior year without him, we didn't even place."

And then Price came along, he thought. Price with his steroids. We're doing well this year, but at what cost? What price for Price? We could all be disqualified.

"Why did Rafe quit? Did he ever say?" Ming asked.

"There was no good reason," Jackson said, casually draping one arm over her shoulder, though he wanted to wrap Ming in both arms again. "He said his image was too important to waste on the track. He said motorcycles were more his style than hurdles and high jumps. He said track bored him."

Jackson took a deep breath, letting it out carefully. Rafe's defection still stung, especially since their friendship had ended at the same time. "I've been thinking about it since . . . since he wound up in the hospital. I nominated Rafe because without him, the team couldn't win. He stole himself from the team, and stole our chance at being state champions. He stole our wins . . . the team wins.

"He had a responsibility to the team. He had a skill. He had to use it. But now I don't know. Just because he could save the team, does that mean it was his duty to? Even if he didn't want to?"

Ming wiped her cheeks carefully with the backs of her wrists.

"I don't know anymore," Jackson admitted, feeling the truth tighten his insides. "I was mad at him for quitting when he was so good. He wasn't just good, he was perfect. But maybe perfect isn't all there is.

"I feel . . . whole when I run," he finally managed to explain. "Maybe Rafe didn't feel that way. I nominated him for a hit because he was better than I am, but he wouldn't run. And I added Julie's name because she . . . because when Rafe bought his motorcycle, Julie dropped me and went with him.

"I thought they were wrong," Jackson said. "But maybe I was the one who was wrong. Do you understand now? It isn't your fault. It's mine."

Chapter 19

Ming was back at school Thursday looking a little pale, but determined. Jackson said hi, and was disappointed at her polite response.

So what did you expect? he asked himself. For her to jump into your arms and never let go? Get real. You are a person who is hoping for a sports scholarship to a decent college, and then hoping you can keep a C average and manage to hang onto the scholarship. She is a person who can get a merit scholarship to practically any college in the country. She is intelligent. She's not going to waste her life on a jock.

He tried to tell himself it didn't matter, but he knew he was lying. I didn't notice it before, he thought. But there's something really special about her.

He went on saying hello to her, when he saw her in the halls, and again Friday morning, listening and watching each time to see if her eyes warmed, or if her smile was broader.

Maybe, he thought Friday morning. Maybe that

was a warmer hi. He almost walked into Brenda, then almost laughed out loud when he saw her. Conditions are ripe, he thought. Yeah!

He shadowed Brenda off and on, and at lunch the situation went beyond ripe to perfect. He watched as Brenda stopped by table after table, leaving behind unhappy, silent faces.

"A sleepover for your seventeenth birthday?" he heard her say. "Oh, gosh! I haven't done that since I was twelve. Sounds like fun . . . in a twelve-year-old sort of way." She moved on, turning back now and then to see her effect in action.

She's like one of those harvest machines, Jackson thought. Only instead of mowing down wheat, she mows down egos.

He looked around to see if Linnie or Ming was in the lunchroom to witness his hit. He couldn't see either of them, but the room was crowded, as usual.

Oh, well, he thought. They'll hear about it. He moved to the sleepover table, pulled the folder out of his backpack, and tossed it on the table. "This will never make the yearbook," he said. "But I want your honest opinion. What do you think?"

The girls at the table were slow picking up the folder, but once the first person had seen the sketches and gasped, the table came to life, eyes brightening.

"I don't believe it!" one of the girls said.

"I do," Jackson said. "I saw it."

"You saw Brenda . . . stealing this bracelet? She has it on!"

That's what I was waiting for, Jackson thought.

I saw her slip it off the counter into her book bag and walk out without paying for it. I just needed a day when she was wearing it at school.

My sketches aren't bad, he thought, considering the fact that I'm a jock, not an artist. He'd done six of them, showing Brenda in stages — eyeing the bracelet, with a dozen pieces of jewelry in front of her on the counter, knocking the bracelet into her bag, pushing the jewelry in a bunch back to the clerk, walking out of the store, and putting the bracelet on her wrist, a smug, triumphant smile on her face.

The same bracelet she was wearing today.

The table erupted in laughter. The girls passed the sketches back and forth, laughing and talking louder and louder.

The noise drew Brenda back, like a moth toward the light it will burn its wings on.

"What is so funny?" Brenda asked.

The girl who had the folder held it closer to her chest, but another girl grabbed it, dropping it on the table.

Brenda picked up the sketches. She looked at the first one, tossing it on the table. The second sketch made her frown. At the third — showing her slipping the bracelet into her bag — she cried out. She threw all the sketches onto the table, grabbed them back up, and looked at the rest.

She crumpled the pictures, dropped them. She glanced wildly at the table, cried, "Oh!" and ran.

The girls broke into laughter. They smoothed the sketches out and passed them to the next table.

Jackson felt his triumph fading. Suddenly he understood how Ming had felt.

Vaguely he heard a door slam and his mind registered that it was the back door out of the lunchroom, the door to the back lot with the trash containers. The sketches made the rounds at the next table over, then were grabbed by someone passing by who stopped, stared, carried them to his table.

"Wait," Jackson said. He wiped his hand across his forehead, thinking, uncertain whether to try to stop what he had put in motion or to let it run its course.

She deserved it, he reminded himself, remembering the parade of hurt and embarrassed people Brenda managed to leave behind everywhere she went.

But he remembered, too, Brenda's face — crumpling, falling apart, horrified, and guilty. I did it to her, he realized. I did to her what she does to everyone else. That should make it fair. Why doesn't it seem fair?

Maybe if I gave her the pictures . . .

He sprinted across the lunchroom and grabbed the sketches from the eager crowd.

"Hey!" someone protested. "I was looking at those."

Jackson stared at the protestor. "They're mine," he said. "And I'm taking them back."

The guy grumbled, but he turned away.

Jackson stuck the sketches back in their folder and headed for the back door. He stepped out, but there was no one there. He stood and listened, but all he could hear was the *ti-ti-ti-hiss* coming from the sprinklers in the park below him. He saw no one.

He waited outside until the bell rang, then went slowly back inside to his first afternoon class.

As Jackson headed for his last afternoon class, he heard a shrill, semihysterical voice near the office. He detoured toward it.

A large crowd had gathered, with the office aide in the center of it. The aide was crying one moment, eerily calm the next as she told her story. "They found her at the bottom of the stairs . . . the ones that lead down to the park," she was saying.

"The sprinklers were on so they couldn't really see what it was at first. One of them said they thought it was a doll. But the closer they got, the bigger it was, until they were close enough to see that it was a person."

"It was Brenda," someone near Jackson said. "Dead."

No! Jackson thought. No!

"I think she was running away from something," someone else said. "I saw her run out of the lunchroom. She must not have been watching where she was going. She fell right down the stairs. It's always slippery when the sprinklers are on."

"They thought it was a doll." The office aide was repeating herself.

Jackson ran from the hall, into the lunchroom, but the back door was blocked off by police banners and an officer, looking solemn and suspicious. Jackson ran toward the front of the school, the story running through the halls and through his head like lava down a hillside and into the sea, flaming and deadly, consuming everything in its path. Brenda . . . dead.

The police had both sides of the school blocked off so no one could get to the back.

Jackson ran up the street and into the park from the front, his mind one resounding voice, screaming, NO!

Chapter 20

Ming and Linnie found him in the park hours later, found him huddled in the woods where he could see the yellow police ribbon — CRIME SCENE DO NOT CROSS — found him staring, staring at the place where Brenda had died.

"It's all going wrong," Ming said quietly, wrapping her arms around Jackson. He felt like a stone to her, cold and unyielding. "Brenda should have laughed off those pictures. She should have come up with some scathing remarks and bluffed her way out of things."

"She didn't," Jackson said dully.

"Things keep going wrong," Ming repeated. "I told you how all I wanted was for Rafe to get covered with food, maybe sit in it, even, and look like an idiot. And he wound up in the hospital."

"She's dead," Jackson said. "I humiliated her and she ran out and fell. She's dead."

"Listen," Ming said firmly. "You're not responsible for what other people do. You didn't tell her to slip and fall. You didn't chase her out here. That was her choice. She could have bluffed her way out of this. I've seen her get away with worse. In fact, if you'd told me what you were going to do, I'd have said don't bother; it won't work."

"I killed her," Jackson said. He shivered.

"It was an accident," Linnie told him. "Now listen. Do you want to go to jail?"

Jackson shivered harder, as if his whole body were spasming. He shook his head.

"You thought you saw her taking a bracelet . . . stealing a bracelet," Linnie said, speaking slowly and clearly. "You weren't positive, so you couldn't say anything to the clerk. But you didn't feel right just forgetting it, either. So you decided to draw the pictures."

"How do you know?" Jackson asked, looking up for the first time.

"We've been busy," Ming said. "Putting pieces together. Guessing. Figuring. Looking for you."

"Why are you telling me this?"

"Be quiet and listen," Linnie ordered. "And remember. You thought you'd show the sketches to Brenda and see what she said. You thought she'd probably laugh and call you a few names and that would be that, but you were hoping she'd get so flustered you could maybe catch her in a lie. You hadn't really thought beyond that."

Jackson looked at Ming, then back at Linnie. "What's going on?" he asked.

"You hadn't really thought beyond that," Linnie repeated firmly. "Then you heard her making fun of some girls at lunch so you tossed the pictures down. It was just an impulse. You felt sorry for the girls."

"I did," Jackson agreed, nodding. Though he knew he was imagining it, he still couldn't get the picture of a too-still, broken Brenda out of his mind.

"Brenda saw the pictures and ran off. You figured she was embarrassed, and you figured that meant she really had stolen the bracelet. So now you didn't know what to do. You couldn't go to the police, even after her reaction at lunch. That wasn't proof of anything. You thought maybe if she had stolen it, you could talk her into returning it, once she calmed down."

"I never thought of that," Jackson said sadly. "It would have been a good idea. Instead, I killed her."

"Don't even THINK that!" Ming ordered, her arms tightening around him.

"And certainly don't SAY it!" Linnie added. "You had no idea she was going to run to the park. You thought she was just running outside to get away from the laughter, and even that surprised you because usually she just bluffs and laughs and that's the end."

"Repeat it," Ming told him.

"Why?" Jackson asked. "We know what really happened."

"Tell me what Linnie said!" Ming said fiercely. "That's what happened!"

"Why?" Jackson asked again.

"Because the police have already heard about the sketches. They know you brought them and passed them out. They know Brenda saw them, got upset and ran out the back door, and fell to her death."

Jackson thought he might never stop shivering again.

"And now," Ming told him, her cheeks streaked with tears, "they want to talk to you."

Chapter 21

It was after midnight when the police finally quit asking questions, quit going over the story again and again. It seemed to Jackson that he'd get halfway through telling it and they'd jump back to the beginning, then jump forward to the end, and he was so confused he didn't know which lunchroom table he'd started or ended at, didn't know for sure who had died. He thought it might have been himself.

But they let him go.

His mother was in her car, waiting in front of the station, her brow creased with worry, her eyes huge, and he had to go over everything again.

"If you don't mind," he told her when he'd finished. "I've heard enough about this and answered enough questions about this to last me the rest of my life. If you would just talk and talk so I could listen and not think I'd be forever grateful."

After a moment's thoughtful silence, his mother started talking about his half brothers, and kept telling stories until they were home.

She cut the engine in the drive, and they sat, listening to the heat clicks of the engine for a few minutes in silence.

It doesn't make sense, Jackson thought. Brenda should have laughed at me. It shouldn't have worked. I don't know why she got so upset, but the sketches can't be the real reason . . . or not the only reason. Something else must have been going on in her life. I didn't kill her.

He said it aloud. "I didn't kill her."

"Of course you didn't," his mother said. "No one thinks you did. Everyone always feels guilty when the police finish with them! Let's go in. I promised the little guys you'd hug them good night no matter how late you got in. I hope you don't mind. They've gotten used to you and your stories, and I'm just not as good."

Jackson sighed, feeling — for the first time since he'd dropped the sketches on the lunchroom table — that maybe, just maybe, he wasn't a totally rotten human being.

Chapter 22

Monday, they met after track practice, all three faces solemn. They met at the field as planned, but wound up on the bottom row of the bleachers, alone, staring soberly at each other.

Ming shook her hair back, then ran her fingers through it as if making sure it would stay away from her face. "It was a surge of people," she said again. "Like . . . I keep thinking about it and I swear it's like someone was back there pushing."

"Rafe remembers hitting your tray with his elbow," Jackson pointed out. "And then falling. He doesn't remember a surge."

"Like a tidal wave," Ming insisted. "Do you hear me? Someone pushed people forward. At least that's what it seemed like."

"I'd say you were nuts," Linnie said thoughtfully. She stood, stretched, then sat on the grass at the foot of the bleachers. "But think about it. I had a tape and it disappeared. I was going to play it at Brenda's party — which would have been bad enough! Everybody was there. But it wound up playing on the school's PA system. How? Why? Who took it?"

"Who even knew about it?" Ming asked.

"I didn't say a word to anyone," Linnie swore, holding her hand up like a Girl Scout. "I didn't even tell you guys. I certainly didn't tell anyone else."

They all looked at each other, Jackson's gaze softening as it crossed Ming's.

"I drove twenty miles to a different mall, and then I told the clerk some story about needing to tape a lecture," Linnie told them. "He couldn't have figured out the whole plan from one conversation! And he's the only one I talked with at all."

"And Brenda," Jackson said sadly. "You guys were right. She fell apart too easily. She should have bluffed her way out of that the way she bluffs her . . . bluffed her way out of everything else. Something was odd."

Linnie picked clumps of grass and scattered them on her legs, then brushed them off. She picked up a few stray blades and began twisting them together. "You know," she said. "It's not possible, but it seems like someone else is involved somehow."

"Think," Ming ordered. "Did you say anything at all to anyone? Maybe someone said they hated Rafe and you smiled funny because you were thinking that his name was on our list. It could have been something as simple and innocent as that."

They sat, thinking, and one by one shook their heads.

"I never showed the sketches to anyone," Jackson said.

"It seems pretty impossible that the clerk where I bought the tape recorder would know anyone who goes to Hollander," Linnie said. "That's the only way I can think of that someone might have known I was making a tape. But it's too farfetched. I don't believe it happened."

"I said nothing to anyone," Ming said. "And I didn't need to buy anything. I didn't need any sketches. I had no help of any kind from anyone. I did make a chart of Rafe's movements, but I can't see how anyone could have seen it.

"Your tape is easy to explain," she went on, glancing at Linnie. "If someone knocked your purse over while you weren't watching it, and went to put things back in and found the tape, they could have been curious enough to take it and listen to it privately. Once they figured out what they had, it could have seemed like too good an opportunity to pass up."

Jackson found himself shivering again.

"It had to have been coincidence and circumstance," Ming said. "Circumstance that caused the opportunity for disaster, and coincidence that it was our three hits that were made worse by the disaster."

"I quit," Jackson said suddenly.

Ming looked relieved. "Me, too," she said. "This is too . . . I don't know. It sounded great to start out with, but it wasn't so good the way it worked out."

Linnie nodded. "It got too ugly. I vote let's officially disband. No more getting even. Julie, Austin, Adler, Karl, and Price are safe from us! Let's all quit!"

Ming giggled. "I never thought it would feel so good to be a quitter," she said. "But I am happy. I am so relieved!"

They grinned at each other.

"Tomorrow let's go get a pizza to celebrate the end of the Dead Game," Jackson suggested.

"And I know what the toast should be," Linnie said. "To Austin, Adler, Karl, Julie, and Price . . . I can't help wishing you bad luck, but I wish that someone else deals it out to you!

"I feel reprieved," she admitted. "Like I should have gotten in trouble, and didn't."

Jackson had been sitting still for a long time. He joined Linnie on the grass, his head propped on his hand, watching Ming.

"Me, too," Ming said. "Though I've never been in trouble. Don't laugh! I wasn't perfect, it's just there wasn't anything I wasn't allowed to do."

"You could break windows and run wild?" Jackson asked.

"I never would have wanted to," she said. "I never wanted to do anything my parents might have said no to."

Jackson sat up, still looking at Ming. "It's a good thing I didn't have your parents! I wanted to do everything I ever thought of doing, felt like doing, or saw anyone else do."

"Maybe my parents weren't as generous as it

sounds," Ming said slowly. "They expected me to learn from my mistakes and make things right if I created a problem. But I had a phobia about doing the wrong thing or making mistakes."

"I never did anything else," Linnie said, twisting grass blades again. "If people are supposed to learn from their mistakes, I should be a genius by now. And I'm not."

"You can't have been that bad," Jackson told her.

"I was, according to my sister. She had the same phobia Ming had about doing the wrong thing. Only instead of being good like Ming, my sister just blamed all her mistakes on me. I thought the family baby was supposed to be spoiled, but no one spoiled me. It was my older sister who was cute and smart and talented. I was the scapegoat." She jumped to her feet, scattering grass debris. "It's time to get going."

They all headed back toward the school, walking slowly, enjoying the fact that it was their last Dead Game meeting.

"I have to admit I learned a lot from my sister," Linnie said thoughtfully. "She put me down to make herself feel better. I realized that people act like that because they feel second-rate on the inside."

"Whoa!" Jackson said. "You're telling me Austin and Adler feel second-rate? They've got the biggest egos I've ever seen."

"To hide how inferior they feel," Linnie told him. "Maybe not that exactly. It's more like somewhere buried inside they suspect they really aren't as good as they want people to believe they are. And in a way I feel sorry for people like that."

"Do you feel sorry for Austin and Adler?" Ming asked.

Linnie smiled slowly. "Well . . . my feeling sorry is as deeply buried as their feeling inferior!"

Chapter 23

Tuesday, Hollander High had a memorial service for Brenda.

Jackson sat hunched, uncharacteristically still, wishing he'd skipped the service. He did smile briefly at Ming when she slid in to sit next to him. He remembered the conversation she and Linnie had had with him in the park the day Brenda died, remembered the feel of Ming's arms around him.

Ming took his hand.

The artistically tempered art teacher broke down suddenly, sobbing. One of the other teachers helped her from the auditorium.

Linnie looked around at all the faces and wondered how many people were genuinely sad about Brenda's death.

Not that they're glad she's dead, she thought. But who will actually miss her? Besides the art teacher. I'm sure Brenda's family will miss her. But even all the people who went to her parties — will they miss her?

She shivered, wondering how many people in the

auditorium would miss her, Linnie, if she died, too.

The thought was sobering.

A handful of people, she told herself. Ten? Twenty? If I died, ten or twenty people in the whole world would actually care and actually miss me. What kind of epitaph is that?

The principal was finishing his eulogy, his voice emotional.

What's really sad, Linnie thought, is that the same is true for almost everyone. Ten or twenty . . . maybe even fifty people if you have a big family, will miss you when you die, and that's it.

Unless you're famous. No wonder people want to be famous! This is a sad way to end things. It would be nice to matter . . . to really do something for the world.

She filed out of the auditorium with everyone else, trying to decide whether to go home, or hang around for forty-five minutes until track practice started and watch.

She could see Ming and Jackson pause together at Ming's locker, talking quietly and seriously together.

Linnie sighed, knowing Jackson still felt responsible for Brenda's death. She hoped Ming was having some success talking him out of it.

I'll leave her to it, Linnie decided. We were supposed to go for pizza tonight, but I think I'll just go home. I don't think any of us are in the mood for a celebration, anyway.

* * *

The rest of the week seemed to drag by. The police evidently accepted Jackson's story, for they didn't call anyone back in for another round of questions. Word was going around school that the official ruling was accidental death.

Linnie, Ming, and Jackson sat together at lunch again, but all three ate silently. Jackson seemed preoccupied and distant.

Ming threw herself back into her studies, reading while she ate.

Linnie endured the silence as long as she could, finally getting exasperated in the middle of the second silent week.

"Will you two quit it?" she snapped. "I'd rather eat lunch with Brenda than with you ghouls."

Jackson looked up. "Brenda's . . ." He didn't finish.

Linnie raised her eyebrows. "My point, precisely. She's dead and she'd make better company. You're alive, but you act like you died instead of her."

Ming looked almost dazed, as if she were having trouble pulling herself back from her textbook.

"I really feel out of it," Jackson admitted. "I can't even tell bedtime stories to the beasts because I used to make up stories about . . . her. You know how I ended the stories? I said in the end Brenda faded so completely she wasn't there at all."

"Beasts?" Linnie asked.

"My little brothers."

Jackson's jaws clamped shut and he looked

blindly at his half-full tray. "It was bad enough that I contributed to her dying, but . . . it's almost like I knew, somehow. That's what I told the kids. She faded away until she wasn't there at all. I can't forget that. And then, what Linnie said the other day about people like that, how they only put people down to make themselves feel better. I didn't realize that. All she was trying to do was feel better."

"Oh, Jackson!" Ming looked as upset as he did. She put her hand on his arm, trying to comfort him. "You helped me feel better about Rafe and I can't seem to help you back. I wish I could make you believe it wasn't your fault. I wish there was something I could say."

Abracadabra, Linnie thought, watching her friends. A magic word that makes everything okay. Nobody's found one that I know of. She looked more carefully at Jackson, frowning at the sharpness in his face. She realized people had stopped by with food, but she couldn't remember if he'd taken any. She didn't think he had. "How much weight have you lost?" she asked.

He didn't answer.

Ming looked concerned. "How much?" she echoed.

"I don't know. Some," Jackson mumbled.

"It has to stop," Linnie said firmly. "You've got to shake this off."

"A dead girl?" Jackson said sharply. "You think I can just shake off a dead girl?"

"Jackson, you were no more involved than if you'd never heard of her and just read about it in the paper. You didn't really know her. You didn't like her. And you didn't cause her death." Linnie jabbed the table edge with her forefinger, emphasizing each point. "Brenda is dead. You aren't. So quit acting as if you were."

Jackson lowered his eyes.

"What about track?" Linnie asked. "Your classes? You're letting everything fall apart, aren't you?"

He didn't respond.

"You can't tell your brothers stories. What good does that do you or them? What good does it do the track team if you act as if you're dead? What good does it do anyone for you to act like this?"

"I know," Jackson said finally. "But telling me doesn't do any good, either. I wish, sometimes, there was someone else to blame. It's so senseless. If I could blame someone else, maybe I could quit blaming myself. I guess I just need some time."

Chapter 24

The next day, Thursday of the week after Brenda's memorial service, Linnie was again hurrying to Studio Art class after lunch, her mind on reaching class early enough to avoid the standard lecture. Gradually she realized that the chatter she was hearing in the halls was a little more excited than usual, a little less subdued. She slowed, moving her attention to the halls, the people, the conversations.

She could tell by the expressions on people's faces that something had happened, so she slowed even more, listening.

"It was Austin," someone said.

"It was not. It was Adler. They found a copy of the test in his book."

"Austin, Adler. What's the difference? You know they both had to be in on it."

Linnie vaguely knew the people who were having the conversation. It didn't matter — she'd have eavesdropped even if she'd never seen them before.

"What happened?" A third person joined the group and Linnie stayed just a few feet in front of them to hear better.

"Either Austin or Adler dropped his books at the top of the stairs. Everything went flying. One of the teachers stopped to help him pick things up and found a copy of next week's science test in with the twin's stuff. And guess which teacher it was? Mr. Byre! The science teacher. It was HIS test he found a copy of! Can you believe it?"

Talk about dumb luck! Linnie thought. Any other teacher might not have realized what it was, but Mr. Byre! He'd certainly recognize his own test! She laughed out loud. Maybe this will help Ming! she thought. If the transfer twins are cheating on their tests, maybe they'll lose their rank. They should get F's for cheating, and that'll bring their grades down in a hurry!

After school Linnie and Ming watched track practice together, frowning critically at Jackson's performance.

"I don't think he's as fast as he used to be," Ming said.

She sounded worried, and Linnie wondered if she and Jackson had admitted how they felt about one another.

"You heard about the transfer twins and the test?" Linnie asked.

Ming nodded. She was leaning on the wire mesh fence that ran around the track, her forearms resting on the metal pole that formed the top.

Linnie noticed that Ming's fingers had curled into fists, but she couldn't tell if the reaction was due to the mention of Austin and Adler, or to Jackson's efforts in the sprint he was running.

When practice ended, Jackson joined them and Ming suggested they go get something to eat.

"Sounds good to me," Linnie said. "And Jackson, whatever it is, we'll cut it up and force-feed you if you don't eat."

Jackson looked startled. "You sound just like Coach," he said. "He got on me, too. But I can't go anywhere. It's almost dinnertime. I have to go home."

"What did Coach say?" Ming asked. "Did you listen?"

Jackson grinned slightly, looking guilty at the same time. "Told me I had to shape up or I'm off the team," he admitted. " 'Eat,' he told me. 'Run.' Life at its simplest, huh? Eat and run. As if that could fix everything."

He picked up his book bag and his jacket, and they started toward the front of the school where they would split up and go their separate ways. Ming no longer walked home through the park, not if it meant going down the way Brenda had gone.

Jackson kept watching Ming and his expression made Linnie want to cry. He looked yearning, hungry, and hopeless. She could tell he hadn't said anything to Ming and that he didn't know whether she felt anything back or not.

Linnie watched Jackson, wishing that someone would look at her like that, love her that much. I just want to matter, she thought.

She shook her head to clear the thoughts away.

"No what?" Ming asked.

"Nothing," Linnie said. "I wonder what will happen to A and A? Do you think they've been cheating all along?"

"We don't actually know they were cheating this time," Ming said.

"From what I hear," Jackson said, "they say they don't know anything about the test at all."

"Of course they'd say that, but who'll believe it?" Linnie asked. "They had a copy of it!"

"Austin says it was planted in his papers after he fell."

"Oh, right," Linnie said.

"I was in class already," Ming said. "I heard the noise and looked out in the hall. I didn't see anyone drop papers in with Austin's, but it could have happened. I didn't see everything."

"I was there, too," Jackson said. "I was getting a drink and the landing was crowded. I remember that. I was thinking only an idiot would put a drinking fountain at the top of the stairs where there's always a traffic jam."

"Did you see the whole thing?" Ming asked.

"Not really." Jackson slowed his steps as they neared the cement benches in the front of the school. "I just heard the noise, and when I turned around Mr. Byre was already helping pick up papers."

"Adler was there, too," Ming added. "I saw them both picking up papers, shoving them all together. And then I went back to class."

"I'm glad they got caught," Linnie said. For Ming's sake, she added silently.

Chapter 25

Friday morning, as Linnie approached the school building, she saw Jackson and Ming on the sidewalk, obviously talking about something important because Jackson kept making broad, expressive gestures and Ming was holding herself very still, staring at nothing.

Linnie hurried, almost running, afraid of something unnamed. Something was wrong. "What?" she asked, grabbing Jackson's arm. Close up he looked worse than she'd imagined he would, pale and shaken.

"Price," he said numbly. "Didn't you hear?"

"Hear what? Did I hear what?"

"Price has been disqualified from everything," Jackson said, sitting abruptly on one of the cement benches near the front stairs. "From the state meet, from the team, from sports, period. Everything."

Linnie glanced sharply at Ming's shocked expression, then her eyes went back to Jackson. "That's bad news for the track team," she said. "Will the team be disqualified?"

Jackson shook his head. "It wasn't steroids," he said. "He'd been drinking. He got disqualified for drinking."

Linnie sat down next to Jackson. "That's actually better, then, isn't it? The whole team won't be under suspicion if Price didn't have any steroids with him. The coach won't be investigated for contributing. Price will get the counseling he needs. I mean, I'm sorry. I'm especially sorry it's going to be so hard on you. But it kind of sounds like what you were wanting."

Jackson got up abruptly and grabbed Linnie by the arm, pulling her away from the crowded front steps. Ming followed them. When they were out of the main traffic flow, Jackson turned Linnie so she faced him.

"That's kind of the point," Jackson said soberly. "It is what I wanted — when we set up that stupid game. And it happened. I just think it's a little odd."

Linnie looked perplexed. "What do you mean?" she asked.

"Doesn't it seem a little too convenient that Austin and Adler, who are on . . . who WERE on our list when we had a list, get publicly humiliated? And then Price, who was also on our list, also gets publicly humiliated."

"I don't think it's too convenient at all," Linnie said. "I think any form of disaster for the transfer twins is simply nicely convenient, not TOO convenient. And as for Price, that just has to be a coincidence, doesn't it? What else could it be?"

Chapter 26

Monday morning, Linnie approached the school reluctantly, almost afraid to see Jackson or Ming. I'm glad A and A got in trouble, she thought. I'm glad Price got disqualified. And it was just coincidence. Austin and Adler were cheating and got caught. And poor Price — he's been using bad judgment for so long it's a miracle he didn't get himself in trouble years ago.

And if all that's true, why is it I'm not very eager to get to school today?

Because something else is going to happen, she thought, looking around at the various crowds of people. Everything seemed normal. Nobody acted too excited, or too serious.

But it's not over, Linnie thought. Not yet.

She saw Ming coming in her direction.

She saw Jackson catch sight of Ming and wave.

"Has anything else happened?" Linnie asked Ming.

"Nothing I've heard about," Ming said, looking brighter, hopeful. "And that's good news . . . as long as you haven't heard of anything."

"Not a thing!" Linnie said, smiling. She felt like cheering.

"I have heard more about Price, though," Ming said, sobering again.

Jackson joined Linnie and Ming in time to hear Ming's remark. "What else about Price?" he asked.

"He says he doesn't know where the liquor came from," Ming said. "He remembers getting off work and it was in his car."

"Where'd you hear that?" Jackson asked. "I haven't heard anything."

"His sister was on the Junior Varsity volleyball team," Ming said. "I used to help coach them sometimes so I got to know her. I called her this weekend. It's been a big topic of discussion at her house, obviously."

"Do you think he's telling the truth, or trying to cover for whoever bought it for him?" Linnie asked.

Ming shrugged. "Hard to tell. It was at least secondhand information by the time I got it. He told his parents, his sister was eavesdropping, and she told me."

"It's inconclusive," Jackson said. "We can't tell from that whether someone set him up or not."

The bell rang and they wandered into the school. Everyone was grabbing papers from the table inside the door. "Oh," Linnie said. "It's the 'Vine." She hurried over to pick up copies of the school newspaper, handing one to Jackson and one to Ming.

"This has got to be the last issue," Ming said. "That means it'll have the Senior Will column in it."

She looked at the index on the front page.

Jackson thumbed through his copy, looking for the column that was a tradition every year. "What did you guys leave to posterity? I left my skill on the football field to Jason Royal so he can dazzle the fans like I did." He found the column, scanned it, looking for his quote.

"I left my soaring artistic vision . . ." Linnie stopped. She nudged Jackson. He glanced up, then followed her gaze. Ming stood totally still, staring blankly. Her copy of the *'Vine* had slipped to the floor at her side.

Jackson, looking as if he'd already heard bad news but couldn't quite remember what it was, reached over and tapped Ming. "What is it?" he asked.

Ming jumped. "It's in the *'Vine*," she said.

Linnie didn't know where to look or what to look for, so she crowded Jackson, reading over his arm.

Jackson pointed to a line in the Senior Will column. It read: *Julie Clay leaves Rafe Gibbons and jumps on the back of Karl DeBerg's motorcycle. It looks as if she's left Rafe for dead and gone after the guy with the biggest bike. Once a flake, always a flake. But will she will her flakiness to anyone? Will Karl leave his sister's science fair projects to anyone else, or is he the only one who gets to use them?*

"You can kiss coincidence good-bye," Jackson said, crumpling the newspaper. "And circumstance. This is deliberate. Everybody on our list has been hit. Everybody!"

He threw the paper on the floor. "Maybe that's the end," he said. "Since everyone's been hit, maybe we can all sleep easy now."

Linnie and Ming looked at each other.

"How did it get in the paper?" Ming asked.

Linnie shrugged, shaking her head.

"We quit and the game didn't," Jackson announced. He eyed Linnie, then Ming, looking stern and suspicious.

"You suspect me or Ming," Linnie said. "That's logical. I suspect you or Ming. If someone kept playing the game, one of us is the logical suspect. One of us did it."

"Not necessarily," Ming said. She bit her lower lip. "I've been thinking it over. I can't think about anything else, in fact. We haven't been as careful as we thought."

"What do you mean?" Linnie asked. "I know I didn't tell anyone. We've been through this before."

"We didn't have to tell anyone," Ming pointed out. "It's all we talked about. We were pretty careful at our planning sessions, but even then we didn't actually check to make sure no one was around. And we discussed it over and over at lunch, at track practice, even on the bleachers. Did either of you look to be sure no one was under the bleachers? I didn't."

"We'd have noticed if someone was around," Jackson said. "Especially if it was always the same person, and it would have to be the same person."

Ming shook her head. "There could have been several people in on it together. And besides, whoever it was wouldn't have to be there every time we talked about it, just often enough to get the names and the general idea."

"If that's true, then they've been watching us," Linnie said. "I followed John Stalley around for a whole week. That's certainly out of character for me! So anyone keeping an eye on us would have known John was my target. That means showing up at Brenda's party was pretty stupid. I might as well have announced what I was doing. It was obvious I had a hit planned, and no big problem for anyone to search my purse, find the tape, and take it."

Ming nodded. "And I did the same thing. I followed Rafe around, and then I stood in the cafeteria every day, holding my tray and watching the OUT door. It was pretty obvious I was watching Rafe, and that I was planning to do something to him with my lunch tray. And even I knew who Jackson's target was because I saw him following her around."

Jackson ran his hands through his hair. "I guess you're right," he said finally. "We were pretty obvious."

"So we can quit suspecting each other," Ming said. "And the good news is, I think the game is finally over. There aren't any names left on the list. We may never know who else played the game with us, but at least it's over."

Chapter 27

"Linnie?" It was Monday night, and Ming's voice over the phone sounded shaken, almost frightened.

"What is it?" Linnie demanded. "Has something else happened?"

"Nothing else," Ming said. "It was enough already."

"Then what's wrong?" Linnie asked.

"I . . . I thought of something," Ming said. "I called Jackson already and he said we should meet tomorrow morning before school. We have something to discuss. Something we didn't figure out before."

"What?"

Ming sighed. "There's something we missed," she said. "And it bothers me."

"What?" Linnie asked again.

"It's Brenda," Ming said. "And the sprinklers."

"Yes?" Linnie listened intently.

"Brenda could hear the sprinklers," Ming said. "They're noisy. You can hear them from the back of the school. Brenda was upset — more than she should have been — and she ran out the back door. We can presume she ran to get away from everyone who was laughing at her and she ran out the nearest door. That makes sense."

"Go on," Linnie said.

"Once she got out that door and heard the sprinklers, she'd have done what anyone else would have done . . . gone any direction except toward the park."

"I don't get it," Linnie said.

"Remember her dramatics in art class, Linnie? She was very careful of her hair," Ming went on. "She was automatically careful of her hair. I just can't see Brenda running toward the sprinklers when the water would have ruined her hair. So why did she do it?"

Linnie had no answer.

Chapter 28

Ming woke — snapping awake — without knowing why. She felt totally alert, yet she was afraid to move, even to turn her head so she could see her clock.

After a full minute of motionless fear, she realized she'd left all the lights on. That awareness helped because it meant she wouldn't have to face anything in the dark, but it made things worse, too, because it meant her parents weren't home. They'd have turned the lights off if they were.

She was alone.

She had awakened for some unknown reason and she was afraid.

She finally looked over at her clock. A few minutes before eleven-thirty. Surely her parents would be home soon.

Home to what? What would they find? What had she heard?

Heard? she asked herself.

Yes. I heard something.

She covered her ears with her hands, then realized she couldn't shut out a sound she'd already heard. She dropped her hands.

What if the noise was just her parents coming home? But if it was, they'd be making more noise now, coming in, turning off lights. Why was a high school senior still such a fanatic about lights and locks, anyway?

She'd had that conversation with herself often before, and oddly, it reassured her. She knew she was a fanatic about lights and locks for the simple reason that she'd been left alone at night since she was little and it scared her.

Of course, she thought, grabbing a robe, they only left me alone because I told them I was too old for a sitter, and then I was too stubborn to tell them I was afraid to stay by myself.

Since all the lights were already on, Ming had only to walk from room to room, checking, and she did, finding nothing and hearing nothing but her heart.

She checked the bedrooms upstairs, both baths, then went slowly down the stairs, listening, certain she could hear something below . . . a rustling flap, flap, flap.

She reached the bottom of the stairs, heard a sudden *whirr*, and screamed, then recognized the noise of the refrigerator compressor kicking on, sounding ten times louder than usual.

Ming took a deep breath to slow her heartbeat, then turned into the doorway of the living room where the flapping seemed to come from.

A drape rustled in the breeze, flapping back against the wall.

Ming almost crossed over to close the window, but stopped, clutching her robe shut at the top.

I closed the window already. I always close all of them.

Then she saw the glass — a hundred shards glittering on the carpet.

She saw a paper-wrapped rock.

Stepping gingerly, Ming bent and picked up the rock, slid off the crisscrossed rubber bands, smoothed the paper.

Just like one of those old-fashioned kidnapping notes, she thought. They always used to cut letters from the newspaper and glue them on the ransom note.

The piece of paper read, *BACK OFF. DROP IT.*

Ming folded the note and put it in her robe pocket, then, even though her mind was whirling, she went to the garage to find the shop vacuum to clean up the mess.

Chapter 29

Jackson woke when the five-year-old beast brother snapped on Jackson's bedroom light and announced, "Your stupid friend didn't have to break the window. I'd have noticed her if she just knocked."

Jackson rolled over and glared. "What are you doing out of bed?" he mumbled, fishing for a T-shirt.

"I hadda get a drink," Wesley explained. "But she threw a rock and it almost hit me!"

"What?" Jackson demanded. "What are you talking about?"

His brother held out his hands, showing a rock, several rubber bands, and a crumpled piece of paper. "It came right through the kitchen window," he said solemnly. "I hadda duck or it woulda hit me. Now there's glass everywhere."

Jackson grabbed the paper. It reminded him of fourth grade, when he and a friend had laboriously cut letters from magazines and newspapers and pasted them on pieces of paper, spelling out every dirty word they could think of and tucking the papers into all the girls' desks.

Only this piece of paper said, *FORGET IT. IT'S NOT YOUR PROBLEM.*

"Did you see who did this?" Jackson asked.

The child shook his head.

"Then why did you say it was a girl?"

"It hadda be," Wesley said. "The girl in the story. Trying to get someone to notice her so she'd be real. It hadda be Brenda." He yawned. "I didn't get my drink. And I'm thirsty."

"What were you doing in the kitchen? Why didn't you get a drink in the bathroom?" Jackson asked.

His brother's eyes opened wider and he looked both amazed and disgusted at Jackson's stupidity. "You can't get chocolate milk out of bathroom faucets!" he explained.

Chapter 30

Linnie woke on time, which meant she was going to be late if she wanted to talk with Jackson and Ming before school started. She rushed her shower, ran downstairs to grab a box of crackers to eat on the way, and stopped short at the sight of her parents, arguing as they swept glass from the entryway.

"What happened?" Linnie asked.

"Vandals, I guess," her father said. "Now I'll be late to work. I have to nail something over this and call the insurance agent."

"I'll call the agent. You just nail," her mother said.

"Nail what?" her father asked, exasperated. "Do you think I keep pieces of wood around already cut to the exact size to fit each window in case one of them gets broken?"

"It wouldn't hurt to have some wood around," her mother said. "I believe it's called being prepared."

Linnie saw the wad of paper and rubber bands.

She picked it up, felt the rock beneath the paper. She slipped it all into her pocket.

"Dad!" she said, interrupting the argument. "Call Mr. Marl next door. Tell him I'll cut his lawn next weekend if he'll watch the house until someone gets here to replace the glass. Then call the insurance agent from your office. He'll know what to do."

She ran off, but not before seeing her father's face light up with recognition of a perfect solution. She felt a warm, pleased glow for the first block, which faded as she jogged on.

Too little too late, she thought. My sister was the shining light. I was just the little lamp that kept burning out bulbs too fast till they threw the whole thing away.

She jogged into the schoolyard and saw Ming pacing, waiting nervously.

Jackson came running up as Linnie arrived, yanking a piece of paper from his pocket, holding it up. "I don't like being told what to do!" he said, his face red from anger as well as from the exertion of running.

Linnie pulled the rock from her pocket and Ming and Jackson froze.

"You, too?" Ming asked.

"Through the window?" Jackson asked.

"We all got one, then," Ming said woodenly.

Linnie freed the paper and smoothed it. *YOU DON'T NEED ANYTHING MORE TO WORRY ABOUT* stared up at her.

She held it out to the other two, who examined her note, and passed theirs around.

Linnie shivered. "I want to go home," she said. "I want to go back to bed and forget the whole thing."

Ming half laughed. "But you have a broken window at home," she said. "Anyone could get in."

"My little brother said Brenda did it," Jackson said.

They all hunched their shoulders against the chill of Brenda's name.

"But he didn't see anyone," Jackson added.

"I wonder if anyone else got anonymous notes last night," Ming said thoughtfully, snugging her windbreaker around her shoulders. "Or if it was just us."

"I'll give you one guess," Jackson said. "We have to face it. Someone is still playing the game."

"I don't want to face anything," Linnie said.

"Me either," Ming agreed. "Let's just drop the whole thing. This is creepy. I don't like middle-of-the-night messages. I don't like broken windows and night noises. I don't like being invaded!" Her hands clenched. "I like boring, peaceful days and nights. I like things to be predictable!"

"Just exactly what do you think the notes mean? What are we supposed to back off from and forget about?" Jackson asked.

Linnie and Ming looked at him. "The game, I suppose," Linnie said.

"We already quit the game," Jackson pointed out. "If you recall, the last thing we were discussing was the fact that Brenda would have run away from the sprinklers, yet she didn't. We were wondering why, and then we all got these notes telling us to forget it."

"I'm ready to forget the whole thing," Ming said. "All I want is my normal life back. I just want to study and do homework and sleep peacefully without rocks through the window."

"You're either missing the point, or ignoring the point," Jackson said. "Somebody died." His hands curled into fists. "We can't just forget that. I was involved in that death. As soon as we started to realize there might be more to it than we'd thought, we got rocks through our windows and warnings to back off."

He looked at both of them, in turn. "I don't like being pushed around. I don't like it when someone I know pushes me around, and I especially don't like it when the person who's trying to push me around won't even show his face."

"Nobody likes being pushed around," Linnie said.

Jackson pounded at the air, too frustrated to speak. Finally he said, "You still don't get it! Put it together! *Why* did Brenda run TOWARD the sprinklers?"

He looked at Linnie, then Ming, his teeth clenched. "I've gone over it and over it in my mind. Brenda ran TOWARD the sprinklers because somehow she was lured there. And now someone is trying to warn us off thinking about it."

"Now wait a minute," Linnie said. "I agree that it was odd for Brenda to go toward the park when the sprinklers were on. But lured?"

"Her car was in the lot," Ming said. "She should have run for her car if she just wanted to get away."

"That's right. Cars offer the best and fastest escape," Jackson agreed. "From school, anyway. So what else can we think? She would have gone toward the parking lot, and since she didn't, I say someone made her go the other way."

"You went out there right after she did," Linnie said. "Did you see anyone?"

Jackson shook his head. "I didn't follow right away, though. Maybe five minutes later. It doesn't take long to fall down the stairs . . . maybe five seconds. That still leaves time for someone to lure her over there and . . ."

"And what?" Linnie asked.

"I don't know," Jackson said. "Somebody knows a lot more about Brenda's last few minutes than we do. A lot more."

Ming looked at him, her eyes dead-sober. "Are you saying someone pushed Brenda? Are you saying she was murdered?"

"I don't know," Jackson said again. "I'm saying there's someone else involved. I'm saying our three hits were a lot worse than we intended, which could have been what someone else intended. We do know someone kept on playing the game once we quit. I'm saying someone lured Brenda over toward the steps. I'm not saying it was murder. Not yet. I need to look at it from a lot more angles than I have so far. It could have been an accident, even if there was someone else there . . . but getting warnings like this makes me think otherwise."

"So now what?" Linnie asked.

"I don't know," Jackson said for the third time. "What I do know is that this is too much. I can't take it and I won't take it."

The school grounds were filling up with people. Jackson stood silently, looking around. Then he walked away from Ming and Linnie without saying good-bye, and without looking back.

Chapter 31

It can't be murder, Linnie thought, trying to look as if she were paying attention in class. There's got to be another explanation.

Linnie kept sinking into her thoughts, then jerking back to an awareness of her surroundings.

My sister started this whole mess, she thought. She should never have told me about the Dead Game. There are a lot of things she should never have done.

Linnie heard someone ask a question, and tried to focus on the teacher's answer, but she kept remembering the summer when she was five years old and her sister twelve. That was the summer Linnie had finally realized what game her sister was playing.

Each summer had two highlights, two special days — the Fourth of July and the county fair in August — days filled with crowds, excitement, food, noise, games, music, carnival rides, streamers, and fireworks. Linnie always had a glorious time.

Linnie had actually believed the accident on July third was accidental. Her sister had run through the living room with her friends, knocking over Mom's antique vase. She didn't notice, didn't stop, so Linnie picked up the pieces and took them to show her sister, who started screaming about Linnie being in big trouble now. She'd suggested burying the vase — had even helped.

Of course, their parents noticed right off that the vase was missing, and Linnie's sister confessed — that Linnie had broken it. Linnie's protests only made things worse. She'd not only broken the vase and hidden it, she'd lied about it.

She had to go to a baby-sitter the Fourth of July and miss the celebration. She was miserable, but at least she believed it was a sincere mistake on her sister's part.

But the day before the August fair their mother discovered money missing from her purse — money that was found tucked into a pair of Linnie's clean socks. Then Linnie knew her sister had deliberately framed her. There was no other explanation. But the more she tried to get her parents to see what had really happened, the more convinced they were that Linnie was making up lies about her sister.

My parents had us mixed up, Linnie thought. *They thought I was what my sister really was. Now my sister's done it again and she's not even here. I wish she'd never told me about the Dead Game, and I wish I'd never mentioned it to Ming and Jackson! The last thing they needed their senior year was to* be caught in the middle of playing a game that doesn't want to end, and wondering whether one of our victims was murdered!

When the bell rang she followed the crowd into the hall, stopping at her locker to trade books. She waved at Jackson, but he didn't wave back.

We're all a little preoccupied, she told herself, settling into her desk in her next class. The teacher started his lecture, and Linnie's thoughts wandered.

I realized a lot of things that summer, she thought. I realized my sister was a fake. Fakers don't really feel, and they don't think. Since they don't feel, it doesn't bother them to hurt other people, and since they don't think, they're impulsive. They just grab at whatever opportunity comes along and then make up a scheme or a lie so other people have to pay for their mistakes.

Austin and Adler are a lot like my sister. They didn't see anything wrong with cheating Ming out of what she'd earned. They wanted it, and they saw a way to take it, so they took it. The same with the others on our list.

Okay, smartie, she told herself. If you know so much about people, use it. Figure out how to get this mess cleaned up. Figure out what we can do.

We have to do something. We can't just wander around accusing each other. There has to be a solution to all this.

She sighed, then remembered she was in class. Everyone else was thumbing through their books.

Linnie heard a whispered, "Page 213," and gratefully turned to the page, paying attention during the rest of the class.

At lunch she sat with Ming. Jackson sat across the room from them and ignored them.

Ming looked at Linnie sadly. "He won't talk to me."

"Same here, I guess," Linnie said. She opened her milk. "I've been thinking."

Ming didn't have to ask about what. She nodded.

"We've got to do something," Linnie said. "I can't think what, yet, but we're the only ones who can do anything, so we have to. We can't go around not talking to each other, being suspicious, and thinking about murder. Wait a minute! I think I know why Jackson won't talk to us."

Ming leaned forward. "Why?"

"Jackson thinks this whole mess is the result of someone listening in on our conversations," Linnie told Ming. "Of someone, somehow, hearing all of our plans."

"So if we don't plan, that person can't hear anything!" Ming said. "I see. You could be right."

Linnie spread her roll with butter and took a bite. "We have to talk again," she said, whispering. "Whether Jackson wants to or not. But we should think things over first. We should look at this from all sides. Get your mind going in some different directions from murder and see what you can come up with."

Chapter 32

Murder! Ming thought, hurrying home after school. She clutched her books tightly to her, as if they could provide a barrier . . . could keep the word away.

Murder.

It's an ugly word, she thought. A big, final word. It means the end of a person . . . the end of all the hopes and laughter, all the smiles and thoughts and jokes. It means an end to function, to eating and drinking, wanting, thinking. Stopped. Dead.

On purpose.

She thought about Jackson, his attentiveness to her, his kindness, his guilt.

Her head snapped up and she stopped, the thought knocking her out of her hurry. Guilt?

He said all along he was responsible. What if he meant it literally? What if he's so sure Brenda was murdered because he . . .

She set off again. No, she told herself. I will not believe that about Jackson.

She remembered Jackson skipping class to make

certain she was okay. She also remembered how guilty she'd felt after Rafe's injury. It's only natural to feel guilty when you're involved, she decided, and that's why Jackson feels guilty — because he's involved — not because he is guilty.

She turned up the sidewalk to her house, noting that the window had been fixed, the new white putty standing out, the manufacturer's decals still decorating the new pane. She fished out her keys and unlocked the front door, remembering the feel of Jackson's comforting arm on her shoulders.

As she thought of him, the pictures flashed through her mind like a slide show — Jackson, always hungry, his look of concern, his almost-constant motion, telling about his little brothers, playing drums on his legs, on the table, on the ground.

I really like Jackson, she thought. He can't be guilty.

And if my mind has to go off in new directions to think of solutions, it isn't going to go in that direction. Jackson isn't guilty of anything except playing the game in the first place. And we all did that.

She felt her face heat up as she recalled how eagerly she'd joined the game, how ready she'd been to humiliate Austin.

I haven't thought about being number three in ages, she realized. It doesn't matter like it used to. Rafe . . . that's what did it. When I thought I'd killed him — that just couldn't compare with something like class rank. The problems are on completely different levels.

So, if I'm not going to think about Jackson being guilty, what am I going to think about?

I got myself into this mess because I was too stupid to see how small my problem really was, and I was too eager for revenge. We didn't really think this through before we started. If we're going to get out of this mess, we've got to be clear-sighted and careful.

She got an apple and a knife, grabbed a plate, carried everything to the table, and started slicing.

Define the problem, she told herself.

Someone died.

No, the problem is more basic than that. That's the result. The problem is, the game got out of control.

What are the factors?

The game players. Known: Jackson, Ming, Linnie. Plus at least one unknown. X. Or maybe X and Y.

She grabbed a piece of paper and a pencil and scribbled the names.

The original victims were: Rafe, John, and Brenda. The intended action (Ia) was complicated by either coincidence (C) or by the action of the possible unknown or unknowns (X, maybe Y). Ia + Rafe × C, or Ia + Rafe × X + Y. Which one?

But there was no intended action for Austin, Adler, Price, Julie, or Karl. We never drew their names or planned any hits.

The equation for the whole thing, she thought, is GOOC. Game out of control.

She crumpled the piece of paper and threw it in the trash. She cut more apple slices.

It's not a math problem, she thought. I can't reduce this to plus and minus.

She thought about their hits. John had come back to school three days after the incident. Ming had witnessed a couple of confrontations between the girls on the tape and John. John had just shrugged and laughed, saying, "There's nothing wrong with going after what you want in life."

Rafe had returned to school after missing three weeks, walking with a slight limp, looking a little paler, talking a little quieter, but joking about the accident. He insisted he'd be back on his bike in no time, and his limp attracted plenty of sympathetic female attention. Plus, Jackson felt responsible since he'd nominated Rafe in the first place, and had begun working at rebuilding their friendship.

And Brenda was dead.

So our hit made no difference at all to John, Ming thought. Rafe shouldn't really have been on the list, and he was hurt. He lost three weeks of his senior year, but he'll be okay.

And Brenda is dead.

Chapter 33

Brenda is dead, Jackson thought, jogging home after practice. His sneakers slapped the letters out on the asphalt, D-E-A-D, D-E-A-D.

For a second he thought he heard an echo, and realized he'd been hearing it for some time. He stopped, but heard nothing. After a second he started off again.

I'm spooked, he thought. Or maybe it was my heart pounding. Death is not my favorite subject.

He remembered when his father died. Jackson had been eight. He remembered neighbors crowded into their house, lots of food, people crying.

Industrial accident.

Things had blurred. He'd seen death before — dead birds, cats, dogs. He'd seen mice caught in traps. But Dad?

It didn't seem possible that someone so big, so good at shuffling cards and cooking stir-fry and cracking dumb jokes could be dead. It couldn't be real. Grown-ups did strange things sometimes, muttering about taxes, IRS, parking tickets, stock markets. This was just another one of those hazy, hard-to-understand grown-up things. It wasn't real.

Not even the funeral had seemed real.

The casket had been closed, and that big black box was not his father. Jackson had been positive his father was not inside. He remembered deciding his father was probably working late, and would come home later. He would be sorry he missed this funeral, since it was supposed to be for him.

But of course, Dad never came home. Things kept on changing, and then one day Jackson was a senior in high school with a stepfather and two little stepbrothers.

And Brenda's death seemed more real than his own father's had.

Because I didn't believe Dad died, Jackson thought. And I know Brenda did. But just because her death is more real, doesn't mean I understand it any better.

He remembered, with sudden guilt, the expressions on Ming's and Linnie's faces when he'd ignored them earlier. I hope they figured out why, he thought, speeding up his pace. The echo he'd heard before sped up, too, and he knew it was his heartbeat, haunting him because he was alive and Brenda wasn't. Her heart would never beat again.

He jogged up the front sidewalk and opened his front door, making it all the way into the kitchen without being mobbed by the beasts. The television blared from the back room so Jackson figured he was temporarily safe. His brothers seldom heard anything other than the TV when they were watching cartoons.

He made a ham sandwich and checked the oven to see what was cooking for dinner. It looked like chicken and smelled Italian.

What went wrong? he wondered. Why does it feel like the game took over and played itself? Like it didn't need us anymore. Games don't play themselves. People play games. Which people, though? That's the question.

The beast-children didn't discover him until dinner, so he had time to think, but he didn't reach any further conclusions. He only reached more questions.

Or the same questions over and over.

Who? Why?

I can't figure it out alone, he finally decided.

He woke the next morning with the same thought. I can't figure it out alone. We have to talk.

Chapter 34

Jackson waited near the front door of the school, waving at Ming and then at Linnie. "We have to talk," he said.

Ming looked relieved. Linnie nodded.

"But we can't talk here and we can't talk now. Somehow, someone knows too much," Jackson said. "We'll have to make sure we don't let him hear anything else we say."

Linnie and Ming exchanged glances, nodding in agreement.

Jackson grinned suddenly. "I almost forgot," he said. "Austin finally found his jacket."

Ming looked blank for a second, then said, "What happened?"

"I heard about it in Phys Ed," Jackson told her. "I guess another guy found the grave and knew it was Austin's jacket. So instead of telling him, he got a few people, including Austin, to help him look for something he'd supposedly dropped in the woods."

Jackson's grin widened. "He led Austin to about

fifteen feet away from the graveyard and everyone started looking. Austin's the one who saw the path and decided to check in that direction."

Jackson shook his head in admiration. "It must have been beautiful! There's Austin, wearing his jacket, staring at its twin on the gravestone in front of him. The way I heard it, he turned all kinds of colors and then ran off without saying a word. He just ran. It sounds like a perfect hit to me."

"I wish I'd seen it," Ming said wistfully. "That might have been the only moment of triumph in this whole mess."

"Where did the new jacket come from then?" Linnie asked.

"It's Adler's," Jackson said. "So simple. We should have realized they both had one, even if Adler never wore his. Austin just borrowed it and ordered a new one.

"But that's not all." Jackson sounded glum. "I heard that Austin and Adler were cleared of stealing that science test."

"What do you mean, they were cleared?" Linnie demanded. "They got caught red-handed!"

"I heard about it, too," Ming said. "Mr. Byre said he had the copies of the test made before homeroom. He took the copies as they were made, put them in a stack, and put the stack in his briefcase. During the whole time Austin and Adler were in the counselor's office, talking about college."

"But if Mr. Byre carried the tests around in his briefcase, then Austin or Adler could have opened it and taken the test later," Linnie said.

"Mr. Byre said he only left his briefcase unguarded once, at the end of homeroom," Ming said. "He went to get a cup of coffee, then came back and remembered the tests. He's pretty sure whoever took the test, did it then. And Austin and Adler have an alibi."

"Darn it!" Linnie said. "I was hoping they'd get F's."

"They do have to take a different test," Jackson said. "They have to take it in the principal's office and be monitored and all, but if they pass, they're off the hook. What's ironic is the hit we thought didn't work at all, is the one that worked best. The jacket."

"They must have a guardian angel," Linnie said, looking disgusted.

"Well, at least the jacket story will be all over school tomorrow," Jackson said.

Ming giggled. "I wish I'd seen his face!" she said.

"Look," Jackson said, serious again. "We can't talk here. This is too public. It's too easy for people to overhear our conversation."

"I've been looking over my shoulder for several days," Linnie said. "But I still think this whole thing was an accident. This is high school. People don't murder each other in high school."

Jackson shrugged.

"It's strange that just one person died." Linnie swallowed hard. "I mean, if we presume it's the same person behind everything, then why would he kill one and not the others? That's why I think it was an accident."

"When Brenda died, we quit," Jackson said, keeping his voice low. "Dying's pretty serious! But the game didn't quit. That's why I think it was murder, because whoever kept playing wasn't bothered by Brenda's death. He kept right on playing."

"Personally, I don't like thinking about murder," Linnie said. "I think we're just talking ourselves into this. We talked ourselves into the game, and now we're talking ourselves into thinking murder. Besides, if someone killed Brenda, what's to stop that person from killing us to keep it quiet?"

Ming's eyes darkened. "We have to tell the police."

"They won't believe us," Linnie said.

"That's the problem," Jackson said glumly. "Especially since I went to great effort to convince them I didn't know anything. I'm not sure how smart that was."

"I don't think it'll be too hard to convince the police we withheld information," Ming said. "The problem will be getting them to believe our new version."

"I'm having trouble believing it," Linnie said.

"I think we have to try, anyway," Jackson said, jamming his hands in his pockets. "I agree with Ming. I say we've got to tell."

"When?" Linnie asked. "After school?"

Jackson shook his head. "We've got the state meet coming up. I really can't miss practice. We don't have Price anymore, so the rest of us really have to work if we're going to have any chance at all. How about later? After practice? No, that's din-nertime. After dinner?"

"I've got a dentist appointment at six-thirty," Ming said.

"We should all go together," Linnie said. "Oth-erwise I might chicken out and not go at all. I'm going to feel like a real fool!"

"I think we need to be together," Jackson said. "For moral support, if nothing else."

"I should be back from the dentist by around eight," Ming told them.

"I do typing for my father," Linnie said. "Usually on Thursdays, but he's got letters that need to be done tonight. It'll probably take me till nine or nine-thirty depending on how many letters he has for me to do."

"How about ten?" Jackson suggested. "I know it's late, but I don't want to wait another day. There's too much chance of more things happening. I think we should do it tonight."

They agreed to meet at ten at the gas station up the street from the police station. Then they would walk over together to tell the police their story.

Linnie started smiling, then she laughed. "That means the game that wouldn't quit might finally be over," she said. "We couldn't end it ourselves, but if we can get the police to believe anything we say, it might finally happen! The Dead Game will be dead for good."

Chapter 35

Linnie ate dinner with her parents, trying to tune out their conversation. It wasn't working very well.

She ate carefully, knowing after years of practice precisely how much food she could take, eat, and leave on her plate without attracting notice or comment.

"Did your Western Literature test go okay, dear?" her mother asked.

I took Western Literature last year, Linnie thought. "Yes, Mom," she said. "It went fine."

"Oh, good. It's such a relief when things are fine."

Things are just fine, Linnie thought. Jackson thinks Brenda was murdered. He thinks people have been eavesdropping on us and . . . wait! We made our plan to meet at the gas station! If someone was listening to us . . .

What if someone gets there ahead of us?

I have to get there first and look around.

"Dad? Can I type your letters right after dinner?" she asked. "I have plans for later."

Her father frowned, then nodded. "I suppose so."

"Oh, dear," her mother said. "You have plans? Your sister is coming over this evening. I was saving the news for a surprise. You won't want to miss her."

My sister? "How can she come over?" Linnie asked. "She isn't here."

"No, dear," her mother said. "She isn't here, but she will be."

Linnie felt confused. "Where is she now?" she asked carefully.

Her mother sighed. "I've told you every night for weeks, dear. I do believe you weren't paying attention. I suppose you have a lot of schoolwork to worry about."

"Where is she now?" Linnie repeated.

"She's been working day and night, I guess, setting up new accounts for her boss. He's expanding, and she gets to move home again."

"Here?" Linnie couldn't keep the alarm from her voice.

"No, no, she's not moving to the house. She's living near that new mall. I did tell you all of this before. She and your father and I have all had lunch and it was lovely and tonight she won't be working so late so she's coming to visit and I'm sure you won't want to miss her."

What a perfect evening this will be, Linnie thought bleakly. I get to go to the police and see my sister, too!

"I won't miss her, I promise," Linnie said. I won't miss her at all!

Chapter 36

The police station was on Delano, with River Street on the west end of the block, and 12th Street on the east. The gas station they'd agreed to meet at was on 12th, up a block and around the corner from the police station.

Linnie drove around the area first, covering three blocks on River and 12th, two blocks on Delano, Eleanor, and Franklin, weaving in and out, trying to figure out where someone would hide . . . if someone were planning to hide and wait for them.

The police station and the library took up the long side of Delano, and Linnie thought the library grounds would be perfect for a hidden watcher until she realized the only place with a good view of the route they would take from the gas station was the library parking lot. It was too brightly lit.

Not there, then, she decided. River Street would be great for hiding on — a person could hide in the trees, or slide down the embankment and wait. But no, the police station isn't really visible from River

Street . . . and anyone hiding there couldn't get to us in time to stop us from reaching the police.

Is that what I'm worried about? she wondered. Will someone try to keep us from going to the police?

She sighed. I'm past thinking what anyone else is going to try to do. I'm just looking for places someone might hide.

She drove on. Both sides of the long street behind the police station were filled with businesses that were closed for the night. Quite a few had security lights on, and their parking lots were lit.

That leaves this section here along 12th, she decided, between the gas station and the corner. She parked near the gas station, cut the lights and engine, and sat, listening to the silence.

It was nine-fifteen. She hoped that was early enough.

She hadn't recognized any of the cars she'd seen on her reconnaissance drive, but that didn't mean much. Cars could be borrowed from friends, grandparents, even neighbors.

She sighed and pulled out her flashlight. She didn't really want to go around on foot checking shadows, but she had to. She'd known she would have to. That was why she'd dressed all in black, from her jeans and windbreaker to the scarf she'd tied around her hair . . . and why she had brought the flashlight.

She climbed out of the car and closed the door with a quiet *thunk*, trying to put together a mental schematic of the area between the gas station and the front of the police station.

Gas station, driveway, pharmacy, street. Medical supply building, driveway, end of police station, around corner, front of police station.

Two driveways. The one by the police station is the back way into the station. A cruiser could come by at any time.

The other driveway?

Linnie slid from shadow to shadow, watchful and alert, using the light sparingly. It was one of those rechargeable flashlights, metal and heavy, and Linnie's arm felt weighted. As she passed the driveway by the gas station, she realized it was actually an alley. She listened for a minute, then continued on, looking closely at the route they would take, checking all the shadowy areas. She paused for a moment in front of the police station. The station and ground lights blazed, bright and cheerful, but Linnie shuddered, wondering what kind of reception their story would receive.

She returned to the alley. She couldn't remember seeing a matching driveway on the other side of the block. Did that mean this was a dead-end alley?

Somehow that possibility made the alley seem darker and more frightening.

Linnie hesitated.

It's getting late, she reminded herself. The others will be here soon. I need to be sure. . . .

She drew in a deep breath and slipped into the alley.

Was that a noise?

She froze, certain she could hear something . . . something like breathing?

The flashlight, she thought. But Linnie hesitated to turn it on. It might show her what was in the alley if she managed to get it aimed in the right direction. What it would do for sure was show anyone who might be waiting exactly where she was.

She left the light off, breathing quietly, trying to shrink into the shadows and decide what to do next.

Her senses felt alive and heightened, her hearing unnaturally acute. Her fingers could feel each ridge on the handle of the flashlight. Her eyes peered into the darkness . . . seeing? Imagining?

She shook her head.

If anyone's here . . . there's nothing moving, she thought. Nobody attacking.

It's my turn, then. It's up to me.

Slowly, working on adrenaline and nerve and determination, Linnie inched forward. She thought she heard the noise again, and fell to her knees, then rolled quickly sideways, hoping to avoid the blow.

Chapter 37

Jackson and Ming both arrived at nine fifty-five, in separate cars but evidently on the same time schedule. Both cars parked and both sets of headlights faded.

Both car doors clicked open, clunked shut.

"Where's Linnie?" Ming asked, shivering slightly as she joined Jackson.

He shook his head. "We're early. She's not here yet. How are you doing? Are we nuts? Do we go through with this?"

"What else can we do?" Ming couldn't decide where to look. She tried meeting Jackson's eyes in the light of the street lamp, but the light fell on her over Jackson's shoulders. His eyes were shadowed, and even in the shadows they seemed too intense, burning.

She glanced, instead, up the street, then down, watching for Linnie.

Her eyes widened. She pointed. "That's Linnie's car," she said. "I mean, it's her parents' car. Who else would be driving it? She's already here."

Jackson looked where Ming was pointing. He nodded. "I've seen her in it before," he agreed. "Unless her parents are here. But that wouldn't make sense. She must have gotten here early . . . but where is she?" He glanced all around them without seeing Linnie.

"I should have gotten here early to look around," he said, hitting himself on the thigh in sudden frustration. "Why didn't I think of that? I'll bet Linnie thought of it. I'll bet she's here, checking around. She's probably on the next block over, hiding in the shadows and watching to see if anyone else shows up. It's what I would be doing if I'd thought of it."

"Then let's find her and tell her we're here," Ming said. "I can't just stand around waiting. I came here to DO something and I need to DO it, not stand around."

"Okay," Jackson agreed. "Come on. We'll go this way." He pointed left.

"You go that way," Ming suggested. "I'll go the other way and we'll meet in the middle."

"I don't think we should split up," Jackson said.

"I want to go to the police station, tell my story, answer a million questions, and go home," Ming said. "I don't want to spend half the night looking for Linnie. It'll be faster if we split up. I will not do anything stupid, Jackson. I will just walk around the block calling for Linnie and meet you halfway around."

Reluctantly Jackson nodded. It would be faster, he thought. I don't like it, but Ming's certainly able to think for herself. It's not my place to go all macho and insist on doing this my way. She obviously doesn't think she needs my protection.

"Okay," he said shortly.

Ming headed to her right, away from the police station, calling, "Linnie?" She turned the corner and was soon out of sight, though Jackson could still hear her calling.

"Linnie?" he called. He took off to his left, hurrying a little so he could meet Ming sooner. "Linnie? Where are you?"

A little way up from the gas station Jackson came upon the opening to an alley. He paused. "Linnie?" he called.

He heard something, but couldn't tell if it was a cat noise or a person noise. "Linnie?"

The sound was not repeated.

It's just a cat, he thought. Or a rat. He took one step into the alley. "Linnie?"

This time there was a definite noise beside him and Jackson spun, his right arm flinging up in an automatic attempt at protecting his face. "Wha — ?"

His question was cut short by a mountain crashing into his brain, splitting it apart into a million stars, into a million Jacksons, each one a tiny glittering spark in the night sky, each one giving a short, strangled cry of pain before fading into nothingness.

Chapter 38

"Linnie?" Ming's voice rang impatiently in the darkness. "Jackson?"

She'd been all the way around the block without seeing Linnie. Now she was almost back where she'd started from and she hadn't met up with Jackson, either.

"Jackson?" Ming waited a minute, then continued. She'd start from the gas station, she decided, and trace Jackson's route, in the same direction Jackson had headed. Maybe she'd missed something. Maybe Jackson had seen something across the street toward the police station and had gone that way. She reached a driveway of sorts just before the gas station, and paused, looking around.

"Hey." The voice was muffled. "My ankle. I fell."

The voice, even muffled, was familiar and Ming plunged gratefully into the darkness, immediately stumbling on some obstruction. She fell onto it, hearing a whistling past her ear as she landed on a body. She screamed, her hand brushing a face.

Ming rolled, drawing her knees up and leaping to her feet. Her heart pounded and her knees felt like Jell-O — the same way they'd felt when she'd waited for Rafe.

It's too dark! I can't see! she thought.

Then her shoulder burst into flames as a great weight smashed it, separating her right shoulder and arm from the rest of her. For a shocked second Ming held her breath, listening to hear her severed arm fall to the ground.

Instead, she fell, landing again on the body. Her right arm crumpled beneath her like a tissue, offering no resistance. She screamed in pain . . . a pain mixed with momentary relief as Ming realized her shoulder and arm were still attached. They wouldn't hurt like that if they weren't attached. The relief faded into a gray blankness as she fainted from the pain.

She woke, feeling motion.

With her left hand she felt for the ground, feeling instead the face again, a familiar face that slid away from her hand as Jackson slid steadily away.

Jackson!

Tears stung Ming's eyes as Jackson's body was smoothly towed from beneath her. Her face hit the dirt of the alley as the cushioning body disappeared. She stifled a sob. Jackson! He's gone . . . and I didn't get to tell him . . .

What?

Ming shook her head. The motion made her shoulder scream.

Shoulders can't scream, she thought dully. But she knew it had, even if it hadn't made a sound. The pain was a scream.

"I'm sorry," a voice said. "But you were going to tell. I can't let that happen. I'll be back after I take care of this."

"Wait!" Ming cried. She wasn't certain whether she'd actually made a sound. "Linnie, don't."

Linnie?

Ming's brain struggled against the pain and the gray, trying to piece the mental images of what had happened into a picture. Her right arm, crumpling onto a body, her left hand feeling a face as it slid from beneath her, a voice emerging from the darkness, a calm voice, promising.

The body is Jackson.

The voice is . . . Linnie.

Ming sobbed in despair. Her shoulder was still screaming without sound, burning, throbbing, and threatening to take over her mind. Pain was the strongest sensation, and it was drowning her.

Linnie.

Dragging Jackson.

With a sudden clarity Ming knew it was true. Linnie was really dragging Jackson away. Jackson . . . limp, unprotesting . . . dead? She felt overwhelmed by despair at the loss of Jackson.

No, she thought. She lurched, trying to get her left arm under her to push herself upright. No. You can't have him.

Her right arm flopped like a dead fish — a

screaming dead fish. She wriggled until she got her good arm beneath her chest and pushed herself back onto her knees, sitting. With her teeth, she bit onto the left wrist of her windbreaker, holding it while she pulled her hand up inside. She let go with her teeth, shrugged her shoulder loose, then awkwardly shook her arm free of the sleeve. She wanted something to tie her right arm with, something to keep it from flapping around.

The jacket worked, more or less.

Using her left hand, Ming pulled the jacket around behind herself, trapping her right arm, clenching her teeth to keep from screaming again as the jacket brushed free of her injured shoulder. From then on, she had to pause frequently to keep from passing out as she pulled her right arm along with the jacket, pulled it snug in front of her body, drew the empty sleeve up over her left shoulder, dropped it behind her, then stuffed the wrist of the jacket into her jeans.

She had a sling of sorts, and had more or less immobilized her shoulder. But how long had it taken her? Where was Jackson now? And was he still alive?

Ming gave a staggering lurch and got to her feet this time with no flapping arm to drag her back down. She headed after Jackson.

And Linnie.

Linnie?

Ming couldn't believe Linnie was doing this, hurting Jackson.

It is Linnie, Ming told herself firmly. She's going to take care of "this." "This" was Jackson. Dead? Or alive?

"Taking care of" either means getting rid of a dead body, or making a dead body out of a live person.

Ming tried to hurry.

Ahead of her, in the streetlight, she could see Jackson's head slithering around the corner, bumping, thudding. Going around the corner in the direction Ming had gone earlier . . . away from the police station. His jacket had ridden up behind him and fluttered on both sides of his head.

Linnie had been facing forward, towing Jackson behind her, holding one of his feet in each hand, towing him like he was nothing but a sled or a downed tree.

Ming hurried, whimpering as she tried to run. Scenes from all the fight and action-adventure movies she'd ever seen flashed through her brain. The heroes always kept going, even with mortal injuries. Bleeding from every inch of their broken bodies they kept going.

Ming gritted her teeth in fury and pain. She gave a low grunt as she hurried her pace, felt her legs gaining strength and spring as she almost ran now, gaining on Linnie, screaming as she ran, launching an attack on Linnie from behind. Ming kicked Linnie's leg, slashed with her left arm at Linnie's head, catching her across the cheek and nose.

Linnie dropped Jackson's legs, turned toward Ming, stumbled over Jackson. Ming kicked Linnie again, kicked her over and over, fury driving her.

Linnie lunged once more, but this time she slipped. Her head struck the pavement; her body fell limp.

Ming grabbed Jackson as Linnie had, but she only had one useful arm. She tried towing him away from Linnie, but the fight had cost her more than she'd realized. She slowed her pace. Jackson was very heavy.

She made it back around the corner and stopped, panting, her shoulder awash in agonizing pain.

Ming could see the gas station, closed, its nightlights shining gloomily against the night. A smaller light on the edge of the station's lot signaled a phone booth and Ming almost wept with relief.

Beautiful phone, she thought, letting Jackson's leg down gently. Dial 911. She hurried, panting with effort. Or is it 0 for operator? Are pay phones hooked into 911? She reached the booth, fumbled at the receiver, knocked it off the hook.

She felt for the dangling receiver, tried to drag it up to her ear. The fight and the towing had sapped her energy, and as the adrenaline drained from her body, so did her strength.

Can't stop, she told herself. Where is the dial tone!

She realized she had the receiver upside down. She tried to reverse it, dropped it again.

"Help me," she begged, fumbling at it again.

Then the world stopped again . . . crashed into her head. Ming was knocked against the wall of the phone booth, slumping, her sight fading.

Chapter 39

"No," Linnie said. "You may not call the police."

Ming could hear distinctly, though the world was gray-black or red pain.

"You may not tell on me," Linnie said. "Do you understand? How can I be famous if you call the police? How can I matter?"

"Jackson?" Ming asked. Her voice sounded feeble to her own ears, her tongue difficult to move.

"I'll take care of him," Linnie said kindly.

Does that mean he's still alive? Ming couldn't stop the surge of hope. "Linnie?" She sounded as if she were three years old . . . felt as if she were three years old. "Why?"

Linnie laughed. "Why? Why did my parents only like my sister? Why don't Austin and Adler think they did anything wrong? Why did Jackson decide we had to tell on ourselves?"

Sight returned slowly and through a red haze

Ming saw Linnie, holding a huge flashlight high, ready. Waiting.

Ming didn't move.

"I'm really sorry about this," Linnie said. "It's all my fault. I should have understood earlier. It was playing the game that made me start thinking."

Linnie waved the flashlight and Ming stayed motionless. She tried to deepen her vision, to see where Jackson was. She felt lightheaded, groggy and weak, and knew she was very near to being in shock.

"See?" Linnie was serious, wanting Ming to understand. "The fake people will win in the end if we let them because the real people have soft hearts. They'll never rise up and stop the Austins and Adlers. Real people can't hate!" She shouted the last three words, then went on in a softer voice, "But I can. I can hate."

She smiled. "I'm flawed. It's okay. If I were a fake person I'd be just like my sister. If I were a real person I'd be a victim like you and Jackson. I'm not really one or the other, and that's why I can do it. I saw that someone had to do it, and I'm the only one who can."

Ming felt tired and slow, faraway . . . fading. She broke my shoulder, Ming thought. And I'm too cold.

"You guys wouldn't even play the game unless it was nice. I could see that right away, so I let it be nice . . . only then I helped it along. All those fake people deserved a little more than you wanted to give them! Then Jackson needed someone else to blame. I figured if the game kept on playing, that would give him someone to blame. But he wasn't happy even then."

Linnie's voice had dropped . . . or else Ming's hearing had faded.

"The game would have ended once everyone on our list got hit," Linnie continued. "I was going to keep playing by myself, of course, but you two would think it was all over. Except Jackson wouldn't let go. I really thought the rock through the window would stop him. It would have stopped me!"

Linnie bowed her head slightly, the flashlight drooping. "Then you two decided to go to the police. You and Jackson will be sacrifices. I'm very sorry about that. I told you it was all my fault, but there's no other way."

We're all so ready to hurt each other, Ming thought tiredly. That's what this was all about. Getting even. Getting back at people.

"It's okay," Linnie whispered. "You won't feel it much. And you'll know . . . you'll know you'll be helping me. We'll get as many of the cheats as we can, Ming. For as long as I live, we'll be working together. We'll get them."

Linnie looked down on Ming. "You'll wait," Linnie said, her voice very kind. "I think you're in shock. Jackson isn't. He's just unconscious. I'd better take care of him first."

She reached over, grabbed the receiver, and

yanked it viciously, pulling it free from the phone box.

The silence, once Linnie had disappeared, was too loud. Ming listened, but even her own heartbeat seemed to have gone silent. Am I dead? she wondered.

Chapter 40

Ming sighed as softly as a leaf falling from a tree, letting go without anguish or thought.

She'll kill him.

I can't let her.

If she'd had the strength, Ming would have laughed at herself — a half-blind, staggering, barely conscious ninety-five-pound hospital case setting off to rescue Jackson.

If she'd had the strength, she'd have wept for Jackson, having nothing better than Ming between him and death.

Instead of weeping, she concentrated. She couldn't take a deep breath — it hurt her shoulder — so she took several shallow breaths. She felt distant and scattered, as if Linnie's blows had literally knocked her out of herself.

Pull yourself together.

Ming knew she'd heard those words before. They came from a past she couldn't really remember, and they sounded like good advice, but how was she supposed to do it? She took another breath, slowing when her shoulder protested, but continuing to inhale until her lungs felt full. She pushed with her legs, trying to grab something to help pull herself upright, and the pain in her shoulder and head acted like a focus for her awareness. If she didn't think of it as pain, it pulsed, like energy, urging her on.

She stumbled to her feet and out of the phone booth, going the same direction she'd gone before, figuring Linnie would not go toward the police station. She couldn't see very well. Her hair kept falling in her face. Shake it back? No. Shaking my head hurts.

She rounded the corner. Stay on the sidewalk, she told herself, because . . . because why? Shapes loomed, turned into a planter box complete with small tree. Ming remembered seeing it before. She edged around the box, feeling more and more vague with each step, feeling like Brenda in Jackson's story — as if she were fading and would soon fade completely away.

She staggered on.

She could hear nothing. She knew the street was lit, but it seemed very dim. There was a certain solid feel to the concrete beneath her feet and Ming felt very wise, knowing she'd answered an important question. Stay on the sidewalk because it feels solid and it leads somewhere.

Her hearing began to return, and she heard sobbing. Someone was sad. Weeping.

Her cheeks were wet. The sobbing was her own labored tears. She stopped sobbing and listened, hearing only a faint rushing of water. Her mouth was dry and her tongue seemed swollen, and the water sounded cool and welcome.

She stumbled into a planter, held onto the small tree trunk, kneeling at the planter's rim. She used the tree to help pull herself to her feet again.

The planter is almost at the corner, she remembered. There will be a street. She made a great mental effort and came up with the name — River Street. The water. The river. The same river that runs through the park where Brenda died. Brenda. Jackson.

The name acted as a focus appearing out of the night, wrapping the fuzz of her thoughts in a form she could recognize . . . Jackson!

She plodded on, reeling onto River Street. She felt off-balance, felt like she was moving too fast for her feet and would fall, but she couldn't stop herself. She almost ran across the street, tripped up over the curb on the far side, stumbled forward for a few yards and fell, jarred to her knees by the little stone wall that marked the edge of the embankment. The river lay below her.

Ming leaned against the wall, her lungs heaving. When she could see beyond her own pain, she leaned forward in horror, seeing the scene beneath her — Jackson, lying on the bank just at the water's edge, lying motionless except for the rise and fall of one leg as it rode the water. Linnie scrabbled around, looking.

Looking for . . . what? A rock, Ming thought dully. To smash his head, then push him into the water where he will float away and drown.

It was almost like watching a cartoon. Linnie and Jackson below Ming seemed only half real. Ming thought she should laugh, but it wasn't very funny. Why wasn't it funny?

She knew her brain wasn't functioning very well. It hurt to think. Bits of scientific information kept floating into her awareness — mass times something, gravity plus something, inertia — but the bits never jelled into a whole.

She will kill him. Soon.

She can see me if she looks up.

Ming sighed herself into the fence, trying to become one with the rocks. Rock. Linnie was almost directly below her, tugging at a half-embedded rock, rocking it side to side to free it from the earth.

Ming could hear Linnie breathing, could hear the grunts of effort as she worked the stone.

Falling object . . . not enough height to reach maximum speed. Still, weight plus gravity . . .

Ming pushed her legs against the ground. I can, she thought. It's all I have left. I can give this to Jackson.

She leaned her good arm against the low wall, and pushed herself up far enough to sit on the wall, her back to the scene below. With enormous effort she lifted one leg, then the other over the wall, stood on the river side of the barrier, and leapt.

She dropped into nothingness, the moment suspended unbearably . . .

. . . until she landed. Ninety-five pounds falling from a height of . . .

They crumpled together, tangling, falling, disentangling, rolling, rolling into cool, damp oblivion.

Chapter 41

Noise and confusion, pain and lights, voices . . .
finally settling into throbbing pain . . . two pains.
Shoulder. Head.

Ming smiled, feeling absurdly pleased that she
had put a name to what hurt. Then pricks and voices
and light, and darkness passed, and more times of
darkness passed and finally she opened her eyes,
feeling human again, alive and almost normal.

"Jackson!" Her voice came out creaky and Jackson handed her a plastic cup full of ice water. She
took a drink.

He smiled at her. "Hi. How do you feel?"

"Okay, I think," Ming said. "You?"

"Fine." He looked apologetic. "Last week I
wasn't so fine, but now . . ."

"Last week!"

"Well, yeah." He drummed on his knees. "It's
Monday. Last Wednesday we decided to go to the
police."

Ming let the missing days sink in. Thursday, Friday, Saturday, Sunday, Monday. What month? April . . . May?

"May fourth," Jackson said.

Ming had a thousand questions, but didn't ask any.

"It was Linnie all along," Jackson said, understanding what she wasn't asking, what she needed to know. "She . . . she didn't plan for this to happen. It started out all right, except she thought the people on the list deserved worse than we were planning for them. She watched us, figuring out what we were up to. She said she didn't really plan what happened to Rafe. She was trying to push her way forward to see exactly what you had in mind and she caused the surge of people. That made her realize she could improve on our hits."

Ming sighed.

"I know," Jackson said. "Her own hit was next. She'd worked with the sound-and-light director for school plays so she'd learned all about the PA system. She played a little part herself, at Brenda's party, making it look like her tape had been stolen, but she had it all planned. She spliced into the system herself and set her tape to play at announcement time."

"Brenda?" Ming asked.

"She thinks it was an accident." Jackson closed his eyes. "She's not real clear on this part. She told Brenda someone had a videotape of her doing something illegal. She told Brenda it would all be made clear soon. She saw me pass out the pictures and she figured since we were near the back door,

Brenda would run out the back door. Linnie went out there to wait."

Jackson opened his eyes, but he stared at his hands. "When Brenda saw the sketches, she thought Linnie was hinting there was a videotape of her stealing the bracelet. A videotape is pretty damaging evidence. She ran outside, saw Linnie, and ran to her. Linnie says Brenda was screaming at her, and either Brenda reached out to hit Linnie, or else Linnie reached out to shake Brenda to make her stop screaming, but all of a sudden Brenda was at the bottom of the stairs. I don't think we'll ever know more than that. I'm not sure Linnie knows."

Ming shook her head.

"The science test was simple," Jackson went on. "Linnie saw Mr. Byre make copies and put them in his briefcase. She waited, watching, and when he left them alone, Linnie was ready. She grabbed one, and then bumped into Austin at the top of the stairs. She dropped the test in with his things and no one even saw her. And the articles in the *'Vine* . . . she planted those, too. She just told the editor she had a last-minute change for her Senior Will, and no one looked at it closely. No problem at all."

"Price?" Ming didn't think about what Jackson was telling her. She just wanted to hear everything. She would think about it later.

"She took the liquor from home," Jackson said, "put it in his car, and made an anonymous call to the coach. And then, the final installment . . . last Wednesday night. She was really afraid I had thought of getting there early. She was afraid I'd be there, waiting for her. I should have been. I was so stupid."

Ming shook her head. Jackson paced back and forth for a minute, and Ming almost smiled. Restlessness, the need to move . . . it was so typical of Jackson.

"When you landed on her . . . I was waking up about then. I saw you fall, saw you both go rolling toward the river. I crawled over and I grabbed your arm. I just let Linnie go. She rolled into the river and floated away and I was glad. I was glad!"

"I would have been glad, too," Ming said. "She hurt us. She would have gone on hurting us. She was going to kill us."

"She didn't die," Jackson said. "She was only stunned. She came to and swam ashore downstream. Some people were walking by the river and saw her crawl out. They insisted on taking her home to dry out and get warm. While they were doing that, I crawled up to the road and flagged a car. The police came. I talked till I was hoarse, explaining what I knew. They believed me, after seeing you."

"Why did she do it?" With everything Linnie had told her, and all that had happened, Ming still didn't know the answer to that question.

Jackson shrugged. "Who knows?" He tapped idly at the edge of Ming's hospital bed. "I only know all this because Linnie's parents told me. They talked to me for an hour, trying to explain what Linnie had told the police and the psychiatrist. They told me he said things about paranoid delusions, delusions of grandeur. It all boiled down to Linnie feeling persecuted, and thinking she could save the world, and being . . . like two people in one.

"They were trying to convince me I shouldn't be angry, I think. I think they're afraid we'll sue them, in addition to all the legal problems they already have now.

"But I'm not angry. I'm just very sad." Jackson looked out Ming's hospital window, looked at the view of the roof on the next wing over. "I've felt like she did, Ming. Persecuted and like I could save the world, and feeling as if I were more than one person. I was big brother, son, student, athlete — and sometimes all those Jacksons felt like separate people who didn't belong together. But I never killed anyone. So . . . what happened with Linnie? She wasn't evil, Ming. Was she?"

Ming's shoulder and her head were throbbing again. She remembered the many faces of her friend, smiling, planning the Dead Game with them, talking, laughing, holding a flashlight over her head, ready to strike, dragging Jackson.

"She wasn't evil. She was just Linnie," Ming finally said. And somehow, that said it all . . . except for one thing.

"Jackson?"

He looked at her.

Ming held his gaze. There was so much to say, about his tenderness, his caring, his attention, the way he cared about his brothers and told them stories, the way he was always so hungry, so restless . . . how could she put it into words?

Jackson looked into Ming's eyes.

You're smart I'm not, he thought.

Ming waved her hand, reading his objections and waving them all away.

Jackson smiled.